Everyman, I will go with thee,
and be thy guide

THE EVERYMAN
LIBRARY

*The Everyman Library was founded by J. M. Dent
in 1906. He chose the name Everyman because he wanted
to make available the best books ever written in every
field to the greatest number of people at the cheapest possible
price. He began with Boswell's 'Life of Johnson';
his one-thousandth title was Aristotle's 'Metaphysics',
by which time sales exceeded forty million.*

*Today Everyman paperbacks remain true to
J. M. Dent's aims and high standards, with a wide range
of titles at affordable prices in editions which address
the needs of today's readers. Each new text is reset to give
a clear, elegant page and to incorporate the latest thinking
and scholarship. Each book carries the pilgrim logo,
the character in 'Everyman', a medieval mystery play,
a proud link between Everyman
past and present.*

Robert Louis Stevenson
in collaboration with Lloyd Osbourne

THE EBB-TIDE
A Trio and Quartette

Edited by
DAVID DAICHES

EVERYMAN
J. M. DENT · LONDON
CHARLES E. TUTTLE
VERMONT

First published in Everyman in 1994

J. M. Dent
Orion Publishing Group
Orion House, 5 Upper St Martin's Lane, London WC2H 9EA
and
Charles E. Tuttle Co. Inc.
28 South Main Street, Rutland, Vermont
05701, USA

Typeset in Sabon by CentraCet Limited, Cambridge
Printed in Great Britain by
The Guernsey Press Co. Ltd, Guernsey, C. I.

British Library Cataloguing-in-Publication Data
is available upon request.

ISBN 0 460 87535 3

CONTENTS

NOTE ON THE AUTHOR

ROBERT LOUIS STEVENSON was born in Edinburgh on 13 November 1850, and educated at Edinburgh Academy and University. He studied law but his main interest was in literature and he had already contributed to various periodicals. In 1876 he made a trip through France by canoe and wrote of it in his first book, *An Inland Voyage* (1878); a later tour, made by land, was described in *Travels with a Donkey* (1879). During his journeys he met Fanny Osbourne, an American ten years his senior who was estranged from her husband. After she secured a divorce in 1879, they married in America. They honeymooned in the mountains of San Francisco which provided the setting for *The Silverado Squatters* (1883). He returned to Europe with his wife and stepson in 1880 and began writing *Treasure Island* which was published in 1883. Its success was a turning-point in Stevenson's career, and he moved first to Switzerland and then to the Riviera in search of a cure for his ill-health. Back in England from 1884 to 1887, he wrote *Kidnapped* and *The Strange Case of Dr Jekyll and Mr Hyde*. The family left England again in search of a more congenial climate and eventually settled in Apia in Samoa. It was here that Stevenson wrote *The Master of Ballantrae* (1889), and *Catriona*, a sequel to *Kidnapped*, (1893). The *Ebb-Tide*, which he had written in collaboration with his stepson Lloyd Osbourne, was published in 1894. Stevenson then began *St Ives* and *Weir of Hermiston*, both of which were unfinished when he died suddenly of a brain haemorrhage on 3 December 1894 at the age of forty-four.

NOTE ON THE EDITOR

DAVID DAICHES was educated at George Watson's College, Edinburgh, Edinburgh University and Balliol College, Oxford (where he was Bradley Fellow). He has taught at universities on both sides of the Atlantic, including Chicago, Cornell, Cambridge and Sussex (where he is Emeritus Professor), and his last academic post before retirement was as Director of the Institute for Advanced Studies in the Humanities at Edinburgh. He holds honorary doctorates from universities in Scotland, England, France, Italy, the USA and Canada. He has written some forty-five books of literary criticism, history and biography and in 1991 was awarded the CBE for services to literature.

CHRONOLOGY OF STEVENSON'S LIFE

Year	Age	Life
1850		13 November, born at 8 Howard Place, Edinburgh, the son of Thomas Stevenson and Margaret Isabella Balfour
1852	2	Alison Cunningham ('Cummy') becomes his nurse and a major influence on his development
1853	3	Move to 1 Inverleith Terrace, Edinburgh
1857	7	Move to 17 Heriot Row, Edinburgh. Privately educated at Henderson's Preparatory School
1858	8	First period of illness
1861	11	Enters Edinburgh Academy
1863	13	Visits France, Italy and Germany with his parents. Leaves Edinburgh Academy due to illness and is educated privately
1866	16	*The Pentland Rising*, a 16-page pamphlet privately printed
1867	17	November: Enters Faculty of Engineering, University of Edinburgh

CHRONOLOGY OF HIS TIMES

Year	Literary Context	Historical Events
1850	Tennyson becomes Poet Laureate; Death of Honore de Balzac	First Public Libraries Act passed
1852	Thackeray, *Henry Esmond* Hawthorne, *Tanglewood Tales*	The Earl of Derby becomes prime minister Napoleon III becomes emperor of France
1853	Dickens, *Bleak House* Verdi produces *La Traviata* and *Il Trovatore*	
1857	Baudelaire, *Les Fleurs du Mal* Trollope, *Barchester Towers*	Indian Mutiny breaks out
1858	George Macdonald, *Phantastes* Dean Ramsay, *Reminiscences of Scottish Life* Ballantyne, *Coral Island*	
1861		Death of Prince Albert, husband of Queen Victoria Victor Emmanuel II becomes first king of a united Italy American Civil War breaks out
1863	Tolstoy begins publication of *War and Peace* Margaret Oliphant, *Salem Chapel*	
1866	Dostoevsky, *Crime and Punishment* John Henry Newman, *The Dream of Gerontius*	Atlantic telegraph cable is laid
1867	Arnold, *Culture and Anarchy*	Second Reform Act passed

Year	Age	Life
1869	19	March: elected to Speculative Society
1871	21	Gives up engineering for law. Enters Edinburgh firm of W. F. Skene and Peacock, Writers to the Signet
1872	22	July: visits Germany; November: passes preliminary examinations for Scottish Bar
1873	23	January: confrontation with parents over his agnosticism; July: visits Sussex and meets and falls in love with Fanny Sitwell, wife of Sidney Colvin; December: first published essay 'Roads' in *Portfolio* magazine
1874	24	April: visits Menton, France; Summer: visits Sidney Colvin in London. Elected to Savile Club. Cruises Inner Hebrides with Walter Simpson
1875	25	February: meets W. E. Henley in Edinburgh; Spring: visits France with cousin Bob Stevenson; July: called to Scottish Bar
1876	26	Summer: canoe trip in France with Simpson. Meets and falls in love with Fanny Osbourne in artists' colony at Grez
1877	27	Summer in Paris with Fanny Osbourne; October: 'A Lodging for the Night', first short story published in *Temple Bar*
1878	28	April: *An Inland Voyage*; June: secretary to Professor Fleeming Jenkin at Paris Exhibition; August: Fanny Osbourne returns to the United States; September: walking tour in the Cévennes; December: Edinburgh, *Picturesque Notes*
1879	29	February: works with Henley on *Deacon Brodie*; June: *Travels with a Donkey in the Cévennes*; August: travels to United States; Autumn: with Fanny Osbourne and her family in Monterey, California
1880	30	19 May: marries Fanny Osbourne in San Francisco; Summer: in Silverado, Napa Valley, California; September: returns with new family to Edinburgh

Year	Literary Context	Historical Events
1869		Imprisonment for debt abolished
		Bedford College for women incorporated in University of London
		First railway across America completed
1871	George Eliot, *Middlemarch*	Bank holidays introduced
		William I becomes first German emperor
		Henry Morton Stanley meets Dr Livingstone at Ujiji
1872	Samuel Butler, *Erewhon*	First University College opens at Aberystwyth
1873	Rimbaud, *Une Saison d'Enfer*	Ashanti War breaks out
		Death of Dr Livingstone
1874	Strauss, *Die Fledermaus* James Thomson, *The City of Dreadful Night*	Benjamin Disraeli becomes prime minister
1875	Death of Hans Christian Andersen	Disraeli purchases Suez Canal shares on Britain's behalf
1876	Twain, *The Adventures of Tom Sawyer*	Queen Victoria becomes Empress of India
		Bulgarian Christians massacred by Turkish irregular troops
1877		Russo-Turkish war breaks out in Balkans
1878	Tchaikovsky, *Eugene Onegin*	Zulu War begins
		Congress of Berlin meets to solve Balkans crisis
1879	Ibsen produces *A Doll's House* James, *Daisy Miller*	
1880	George Newnes starts *Tit-Bits* de Maupassant publishes his first stories in *Boule de Suif*	William Ewart Gladstone becomes prime minister

Year	Age	Life
1881	31	April: Davos, Switzerland. *Virginibus Puerisque*; Summer: France and Scotland
1882	32	February: *Familiar Studies of Men and Books*; April: moves to Davos, Switzerland; June: returns to Scotland; July: *New Arabian Nights*; Autumn: moves to France, Marseilles and Nice; December: first performance of *Deacon Brodie* in Bradford
1883	33	March: settles at Chalet La Solitude, Hyères, France; November: *Treasure Island*
1884	34	January: *Silverado Squatters*. Further illness; Autumn: moves back to England following outbreak of cholera at Hyeres.
1885	35	Spring: settles at Skerryvore, Bournemouth; Friendship with Henry James and Walter Besant; March: *A Child's Garden of Verses*; April: *More Arabian Nights* and *The Dynamiter*; November: *Prince Otto*
1886	36	January: *The Strange Case of Dr Jekyll and Mr Hyde*; July: *Kidnapped*
1887	37	February: *The Merry Men*; May: Thomas Stevenson dies in Edinburgh; July: *Underwoods*; August: sails for United States and settles at Saranac Lake; November: *Memories and Portraits*
1888	38	January: *Memoir of Fleeming Jenkin*; April: moves to New York and New Jersey. Meets Mark Twain. Quarrels with Henley; June: *The Black Arrow*. Sets out on first Pacific voyage to Marquesas on board the Casco
1889	39	January: stays in Hawaii; June: *The Wrong Box* (with Lloyd Osbourne). Second Pacific voyage to the Gilbert Islands on board the Equator; September: *The Master of Ballantrae*; December: visits Samoa and purchases land

Year	Literary Context	Historical Events
1881	Death of Thomas Carlyle	Death of Disraeli First Boer War breaks out Alexander III becomes Tsar of Russia
1882	Publication begins of *Dictionary of National Biography*	Married Woman's Property Act passed Pretoria Convention ends Boer War Triple Alliance formed between Italy, Austria and Germany
1883	Birth of Compton Mackenzie Death of Edward Fitzgerald, author of *The Rubaiyat of Omar Khayyam*	
1884	Publication begins of the *Oxford English Dictionary*	Fabian Society founded Third Reform Act passed
1885		Earl of Salisbury becomes prime minister Death of General Charles Gordon at Khartoum Death of General Ulysses S. Grant
1886	Hardy, *The Mayor of Casterbridge* Death of Emily Dickinson	First Irish Home Rule Bill fails
1887	Birth of Edwin Muir Arthur Conan Doyle publishes the first Sherlock Holmes story, *A Study in Scarlet*	Queen Victoria's Golden Jubilee
1888	August Strindberg produces *Miss Julie*	Jack the Ripper murders six women in London John Boyd Dunlop produces pneumatic tyres William II becomes German emperor
1889	Death of Gerard Manley Hopkins W. B. Yeats, *The Wanderings of Oisin* J. M. Barrie, *A Window in Thrums*	First London dock strike

Year	Age	Life
1890	40	February: visits Sydney, Australia; April: Third voyage to Gilbert and Marshall islands on board the *Janet Nichol*; July: *Father Damien*; October: settles in Samoa and builds Vailima; December: *Ballads*
1891	41	Mother arrives in Samoa
1892	42	April: *Across the Plains*; June: *The Wrecker*; August: *A Footnote to History*
1893	43	January: Vailima completed; April: *Island Nights' Entertainments*; September: *Catriona*
1894	44	September: *The Ebb-Tide*; 3 December: Dies of cerebral haemorrhage at Vailima, Samoa
1895		January: *The Amateur Emigrant* (revised text of 1880 edition); October: *Vailima Letters*
1896		March: *Fables*; May: *Weir of Hermiston*; August: *Songs of Travel*; September: *In the South Seas*
1897		October: *St Ives*
1899		*Letters to His Family and Friends*, edited by Sidney Colvin

Year	Literary Context	Historical Events
1890		Bismarck is dismissed as chancellor
		Parnell/O'Shea divorce case
		Henri de Toulouse-Lautrec produces first Moulin Rouge paintings
1891	Birth of Neil Gunn	Elementary school fees abolished
		Paul Gauguin settles in Tahiti
1892	Oscar Wilde produces *Lady Windermere's Fan*	
	Birth of Hugh MacDiarmid	
1893	Sir Arthur Wing Pinero produces *The Second Mrs Tanqueray*	Matabele rising
		Second Irish Home Rule Bill fails
		Civil war breaks out in Samoa
1894	Kipling, *The Jungle Book*	Death of Louis Kossuth
	John Buchan publishes his first book, *Essays and Apothegms of Francis Lord Bacon*	Earl of Rosebery becomes prime minister
	du Maurier, *Trilby*	
	Gissing, *In the Year of Jubilee*	
	George Moore, *Esther Waters*	
	Hope, *The Prisoner of Zenda*	

INTRODUCTION

ROBERT LEWIS BALFOUR STEVENSON was born in Edinburgh in 1850. (His father soon changed the spelling 'Lewis' to 'Louis', but the final 's' was always pronounced by his family and friends.) His father was a lighthouse engineer, of a distinguished family of lighthouse engineers, and Louis was expected to follow the family profession. He was often ill as a child with pulmonary complaints, and as he lay in bed playing with toy soldiers and imagining picturesque scenes and incidents his imagination developed with remarkable precocity. Although he grew up in Edinburgh's elegant New Town he was well aware of the less salubrious areas of the city and of the contrast between Presbyterian self-righteousness and the lives and manners of the poor and disreputable. He entered Edinburgh University in November 1867, ostensibly to study engineering but in fact determined to pursue a literary career. After a showdown with his father it was agreed that he should study law and pursue literature as an avocation, and although he did take a law degree it soon became clear – and it was eventually accepted by his family – that his profession was to be that of writer. He practised from an early age, imitating, exploring, trying his hand at a variety of styles, experimenting, listening to rhythms and cadences, showing off sometimes, but always conscious of his aim as a literary artist.

As a student Stevenson explored the bohemian aspects of Edinburgh city life and with deliberate bravado set the bohemian ideal against the stern moralism of the Presbyterian tradition in which he was brought up. Yet he was essentially a moralist, never wholly escaping from his Calvinist background, and his bohemian gestures as a young man were made as a matter of principle, protesting against what he considered to be the

sanctimonious hyprocisy of the respectable citizens of Edinburgh. In fact the bohemian and the Calvinist co-existed in
Stevenson's make-up all his life. When his father, a passionate
Christian in a somewhat eccentric mode, discovered his son's
rebellious views on religion and morality he was deeply shaken,
and young Stevenson found himself involved in a bitter quarrel
with a parent he loved and admired in spite of their differences.
This resulted in a preoccupation with father-son relations that
can be traced right through his work to his unfinished masterpiece *Weir of Hermiston*. He was deeply concerned with the
moral ambiguities of the human animal, with the co-existence of
good and evil in everyone, and while he produced in *The Strange
Case of Dr Jekyll and Mr Hyde* the most obvious treatment of
this subject, it can be seen almost everywhere else in his work.

Soon after this crisis with his parents Stevenson had to go
abroad for his health. His frequent respiratory complaints, his
spitting of blood and bouts of almost total physical incapacity,
which continued at intervals throughout his life until he finally
settled in the South Seas, meant that he frequently had to leave
Scotland, a country he loved, for places farther south. It was
while living in an artists' colony in Fontainebleau – his cousin
R. A. B. Stevenson ('Bob'), an artist and art critic, had introduced him there – that he met Fanny van de Grift Osbourne, an
American separated from her husband. They fell in love and in
1879 Stevenson followed her to California where, after Fanny's
divorce, they married. A reconciliation with his parents and a
happy return to Scotland – where he began *Treasure Island* in a
cottage in Braemar – were followed by further attacks of
respiratory trouble and he and Fanny moved to Davos, Switzerland, thought to be a healthy place for consumptives (although
it now appears likely that Stevenson never suffered from tuber-
culosis but from another chest disease, bronchiectasis, which
often begins in childhood following pneumonia, whooping
cough or repeated acute episodes of bronchitis). In 1883 the
Stevensons were living in Hyères in the south of France, and in
1884 they settled in Bournemouth – the south coast of England
being considered a reasonably good climate for Louis – in a

house given to Fanny by Stevenson's father as a wedding present. There he wrote *The Strange Case of Dr Jekyll and Mr Hyde* as well as *Kidnapped*, and found himself famous.

The death of Stevenson's father in 1887 left him free to leave Britain, and in August of that year the Stevensons left the country never to return (although they did not know this then). Stevenson was in search of health. After a stay at Saranac in the Adirondack Mountains – then regarded as a sovereign place for the tubercular – where he worked on *The Master of Ballantrae*, Stevenson developed a plan of a long sea voyage which he thought would be beneficial to his health. Fanny, visiting relatives in the west, discovered in San Francisco that the yacht *Casco* was available for hire, with Captain Otis in command, for a trip among the islands of the South Seas. Stevenson jumped at the opportunity. On 27 May 1888 he wrote to Henry James: 'On June 15th the schooner yacht *Casco* will (jealous providence permitting) steam through the Golden Gates for Honolulu, Tahiti, the Galapagos, Guayaquil, and – I hope *not* the bottom of the Pacific. It will contain your obedient 'umble servant and party. It seems too good to be true . . .'

Thus began Stevenson's devotion to the South Seas, which lasted for the rest of his short life (he died suddenly of a cerebral haemorrhage on 3 December 1894 in 'Vailima', the house he had built for himself and his family in Apia, Samoa). In this climate he was well and active. When he left – as he did to visit Australia – he was stricken with sudden grave illness again. He was in best health of all when voyaging on the sea, and he took several long trips, including a cruise aboard the *Janet Nicoll* to the Gilbert, Marshall and other islands in April–August 1890, getting to know native chiefs and customs, studying the history, politics and anthropology of the islands, taking a serious interest in native culture and defending it against the destructive influence of unimaginative missionaries. He wrote letters to *The Times* criticizing the politics of the Great Powers with respect to the Pacific Islands. He became known and loved throughout the South Seas as the great Tusitala, story-teller, and friend of the islanders. And his health remained stable, as it had never done before. He had to explain to his friends in Britain why he was not coming home. 'I feel as if I were untrue to friendship,' he wrote to Sidney Colvin in April 1889, '. . . but I think you will pardon me if you consider how much this tropical weather mends my health. Remember me as I was at home, and think of me sea-bathing and walking about, jolly as a sandboy: you will own the temptation is strong; and as the scheme, bar fatal accidents, is bound to pay into the bargain, sooner or later, it seems it would be madness to come home now.'

Stevenson wrote to his former physician, Dr Scott, from Samoa in January 1880: 'I have now been some twenty months in the South Seas, and am (up to date) a person whom you would scarcely know. I think nothing of long walks and rides: I was four hours and a half gone the other day, partly riding, partly climbing up a steep ravine. I have stood a six months voyage on a copra schooner with about three months ashore on coral atolls, . . . I am so pleased with the climate that I have decided to settle.'

Yet his imagination was haunted by his native Scotland, and he never wrote more movingly about Scottish place and character than he did in the works he wrote in the South Pacific. At the same time, he noted with the discerning eye of the writer, the moralist, the psychologist and indeed the anthropologist the reality of life in the South Seas both for the natives and for the incomers. Like his younger contemporary Joseph Conrad, he observed the impact of European traders and adventurers on the native culture with deep unease, and saw how the lure of the tropics could draw out both the best and the worst in the incomers. For the remittance man, the beachcomber or the adventurer the lure of the tropics could be sinister: it could corrupt the best and attract the worst. Conrad was concerned with the power of darkest Africa to destroy the white intruder, both the rogue and (even more so) the idealist, as he shows with enormous power in *Heart of Darkness* and, more directly, if in a slighter manner, in *An Outpost of Progress*. Stevenson's aim was in a way more subtle: it was both to show how the tropics attract and exacerbate European occupation and how the unconscious assumptions of racial superiority can produce either outright evil or a queer, ironic kind of good. Both are shown in Stevenson's late masterpiece *The Beach at Falesá*. *The Ebb-Tide*, the other remarkable product of this new turn in Stevenson's genius, is a grim story of moral failure counterpointed against a particular island landscape, seascape and atmosphere. The South Seas here act as magnet as well as crucible.

The Ebb-Tide was written in conjunction with Stevenson's stepson Lloyd Osbourne, but although Osbourne did some of the original drafting of the opening, the story as we have it is essentially Stevenson's and, while he put Lloyd's name on the title-page as co-author, in his letters he nearly always refers to it as simply his. He wrote to the novelist S. R. Crockett from Vailima on 17 May 1893: 'Yes, honestly, fiction is very difficult, it is a terrible strain to *carry* your characters all that time. And the difficulty of according the narrative and the dialogue (in a work in the third person) is extreme. That is one reason why I so often prefer the first. It is much on my mind just now, because of my last work, just off the stocks three days ago, *The Ebb Tide*. It is a dreadful, grimy business in the third person, where the strain between a vilely realistic dialogue and a narrative style pitched about (in phrase) "four notes higher" than it should have been has sown my head with gray hairs; or I believe so – if my head has escaped, my heart has them.' Stevenson continues, in a way that both makes clear that *The Ebb-Tide* is essentially his and illuminates its place in his career as a writer: 'The truth is, I have a little lost my way, and stand bemused at the crossroads. A subject? Ay, I have dozens, I have at least four novels begun, they are none good enough; and the mill waits, and I'll have to take second best. *The Ebb-Tide* I make the world a present of; I expect, and, I suppose, deserve to be torn to pieces; but there was all that good work lying useless, and I had to finish it.'

Stevenson was aware that he was at a critical phase in his career as a writer, moving away from his earlier concept of romance towards something more contemporary and more

grimly realistic yet at the same time not abandoning his earlier
vein, as the several works he left unfinished at his sudden death
clearly show. He was experimenting with a variety of different
modes, and while in this letter he expressed some dissatisfaction
with *The Ebb-Tide* this reflected his standing 'bemused at the
cross-roads' rather than real dissatisfaction. We know that he
thought well of its companion piece, *The Beach at Falesá*, for he
wrote to Henry James that its art 'seems to me an art brought
to perfection and I delight in the observed truth, the modesty of
nature, of the narrator.' Of *The Ebb-Tibe* he wrote to Henry
James more defensively: 'My dear man, the grimness of that
story is not to be depicted in words. There are only four
characters, to be sure. But what a troop of swine! And their
behaviour is really so beneath any possible standard, that on a
retrospect I wonder I have been able to endure them myself until
the yarn was finished. Well, there is always one thing; it will
serve as a touchstone. If the admirers of Zola admire him for his
pertinent ugliness and pessimism, I think they should admire
this; but if, as I have long suspected, they neither admire nor
understand the man's art, and only wallow in his rancidness like
a hound in offal, then they will certainly be disappointed in *The
Ebb Tide*. Alas! poor little tale, it is not *even* rancid.'

The original title was to have been *The Pearl Fisher*, and then
Stevenson changed the title to *The Schooner Fallarone*. He wrote
to his old Edinburgh friend Charles Baxter on 1 March 1893
that it was 'a most grim and gloomy tale'. It was 'the butt end
of what once was *The Pearl Fisher* ... We have been rather
tempted to call it *The Schr. Fallarone: A Tract by R. L. S. and
L. O.* It would make a boss [excellent] tract: the three main
characters – and there are only four – are barrats, insurance
frauds, thieves, and would-be murderers; so the company's
good. Devil a woman there, by good luck: so it's pure! 'Tis a
most – what's the expression? – unconventional work.' A few
months later he wrote again about the story to Baxter, calling it
'that Grimy Work'.

The story opens on Papeete beach, in the Society Islands,
which Stevenson first saw in September 1888, having arrived in

the *Casco* from Fakarava in Paumotu (or Tuamotu or Low Archipelago). The archipelago was annexed by France in 1881, forming part of the dependency of Tahiti, as did the Society Islands. 'Get out your big atlas,' wrote Stevenson to Colvin from Fakarava on 21 September 1888, 'and imagine a straight line from San Francisco to Anaho, the N. E. corner of Nukahiva, one of the Marquesas Islands; imagine three weeks there: imagine a day's sail on August 12th round the eastern end of the island to Tai-o-hae, the capital; imagine us there till August 22nd: imagine us skirt the east side of Ua-pu – perhaps Roana-Poa on your atlas – and through the Bondelais straits to Taaka-uku in Hive-Oa, where we arrive on the 23rd; imagine us there until September 4th, when we sailed for Fakarava, which we reached on the 9th, after a very difficult and dangerous passage among these isles. Tuesday, we shall leave for Tahiti, ... I did not dream there were such places or such races.'

In his South Pacific voyages Stevenson was to get to know the places and races much better. He relished the Polynesian place names, gradually acquired something of the language, and found on the beaches the perfect setting for two of his stories. Writing in November from Tautira, virtually adjoining Papeete on the peninsula of Tahiti in the Society Islands, he calls the place 'the Garden of the world', 'Tautira being mere Heaven'. They had to spend two months there while the *Casco*'s rotten mainmast was replaced. Here he planned a South Sea travel book. On 14 January 1889 he wrote to Colvin from the *Casco* 'at sea, twenty days out from Papeete', full of stories of life in Tautira. It must have been at this time that the theme of *The Ebb-Tide* first formed itself in his mind. He had already begun to observe and meditate on the mixed fortunes of the white man in Polynesia and their relation to the moral and psychological paradoxes that continued to haunt him.

So *The Ebb-Tide* begins 'on the beach', a phrase that, as Stevenson had learned, was used with reference to stranded and destitute white men in Polynesia. The opening sentence gives notice that Stevenson, like Conrad, was concerned with the ambivalent role of the white man in the tropics. 'Throughout the island world of the Pacific, scattered men of many European races carry activity and disseminate disease.' The calm deadpan of the conjunction of activity and disease is part of that third-person narrative style that Stevenson found so demanding. The descriptive tone varies with the movement of the story. The account of the *Fallarone* making landfall on the shore of the unknown island is full of the sense of beauty and excitement that Stevenson's own letters show in describing such scenes. Yet it is against the beauty of the physical scene, the challenge of the ocean, the demands of seamanship, that the 'grimness' of the story so much emphasised by Stevenson in his account of it in his correspondence, is deployed. Everything is anchored in vividly particularised local scenery, from the three men 'seated on the beach under a *purao* tree' with 'the moon racing through a world of flying clouds of every size and shape and density' to the precarious boarding of the *Fallarone*, changes in weather, the sudden squall and its effects, and the precisely pictured description of Attwater's island and what was on it. Conrad's scenery is often darkly symbolic: 'An empty stream, a great silence, an impenetrable forest. The air was warm, thick, heavy, sluggish . . . It was the stillness of an implacable force brooding over an inscrutable intention.' Stevenson did not go in for such abstractions. He sets his grimy characters in vividly visualised scenes: the scenery does not, as in Conrad, comment on the moral abyss he is exploring. Neither landscape nor seascape is psychological: they are vivid, colourful, and portrayed with relish. This makes his exploration of his characters starker and in a way more terrible. They do not share in a corrupt natural background, rather they stand in contrast to a background of innocent – indeed glorious – nature.

Of the three characters introduced on the beach, one is an Oxford-educated English gentleman whose decline into a Polynesian beachcomber is perhaps the least convincing in its psychological perception. Sensitive, humane and literate, Robert Herrick is presented as having had a career of 'unbroken shame', but the reason for his decline, his deficiency 'in consistency and in intellectual manhood', is never fully explored. He has more obvious redeeming features than his two companions, and when he refers to Beethoven's Fifth Symphony or quotes Virgil the reader can see a kind of snobbish cultural assurance behind the degenerate façade. Herrick, like all the characters in the story, and like so many other characters in Stevenson's fiction, is a study in moral ambivalence. Davis, the disgraced sea captain who lost his ship and passengers through drunkenness, is in spite of his all too obvious failings and stupidly drunken behaviour as master of the *Fallarone* a not wholly unattractive character, with moments of softness and even of dignity. Even the degenerate Cockney clerk Huish, the most morally contemptible of the three, has a kind of wit and possesses real courage. Attwater, strong, determined, intelligent, masterful, is at the same time a cruel fanatic. 'A troop of swine'? It is interesting that in his correspondence with friends Stevenson is at pains to emphasise the total moral degeneracy of his four characters. But in fact the moral situation is much subtler than that, and as different facets of each character are exposed the ambiguities emerge. The mutual recognition of educated gentlemanliness between Herrick and Attwater is both an exposure of upper-class English cultural snobbery and an assertion of Stevenson's own high culture. One of the few books Stevenson had with him on the *Casco* was Virgil's *Aeneid* (in Latin, with no Latin dictionary), and he makes use of Virgil to establish both Herrick's cultural superiority to his two companions (he quotes Virgil to them and they don't understand) and his cultural communion with Attwater (when Attwater calls the island *nemerosa Zacynthos*, 'wooded Zacynthos', Herrick completes the Virgilian line with *Iam medio apparet fluctu*, 'now appears in the midst of the flood'). In his comments on his characters to his friends Stevenson deliberately and defensively oversimplifies them. They are all, of course, villains in one way or another, thieves, swindlers and would-be murderers, but not only are there significant moral differences between them there is also a subtle relationship between their vices and their suppressed or lost or potential virtues. Herrick has sensitivity, Davis retains (at moments) a certain dignity and pride, Huish has his own

kind of indomitableness and courage, Attwater has his honesty
and integrity. If in one way or another they are all damned, they
are not – not even Huish, easily the worst of the bunch – *simply*
damned.

Behind all the action and behind the dilemmas facing the
characters lie the islands and their native inhabitants. The
attitudes of Herrick, Davis and Huish to the crew are clearly
distinguished. The dark African who calls himself Sally Day is
treated with friendly contempt by Davis. 'Didn't know we had
ladies on board. Well, Sally, oblige me by hauling down that rag
there.' The Kanakas (Polynesian natives) who make up most of
the crew are also treated by Davis with good-natured contempt.
' "What's your name?" says the captain, "what's that you say?,
that's not English. We'll call you old Uncle Ned, because you've
got no wool on top of your head, just the place where the wool
ought to grow" ' (a quotation from a once-popular song about
a black American). After one of the Kanaka crew jumped into
the sea and swam ashore, Davis was ruthlessly in command
' "Anybody else for shore?" he cried, and the savage trumpeting
of his voice, no less than the ready weapon in his hand, struck
fear in all.' Herrick's moral stature, in spite of all his degrada-
tion, is established in his relation with Uncle Ned:

> "He tell you tlue," said Uncle Ned. "You sleep. Evely man hea
> he do all light. Evely man he like you too much."
> Herrick struggled, and gave way; choked upon some trivial
> words of gratitude; and walked to the side of the house, against
> which he leaned, struggling with emotion.
> Uncle Ned presently followed him and begged him to lie down.
> "It's no use, Uncle Ned," he replied. "I couldn't sleep. I'm
> knocked over with all your goodness."
> "Ah, no call me Uncle Ned no mo'!" cried the old man. "No
> my name! My name Taveeta all-e-same Taveeta King of Islael.
> Wat for he call me that Hawaii? I think no savvy nothing . . ."

And Uncle Ned tells Herrick the truth about the ship's former
captain.

This is one of the moral centres of the story. Herrick makes
real human contact with one of the natives in his true identity,
and learns the unedifying truth about the late captain of the

Fallarone. Throughout the whole story the characters circle around one another, adopting and discarding poses, confessing, boasting, blustering, lying, acting, but in the exchange between Herrick and Uncle Ned we get a rare moment of truth.

The Kanakas are everywhere in the background. Attwater dominates and uses them. Davis and Huish take them for granted as a convenient workforce and part of the scenery. Herrick alone has the occasional awareness of their human reality. *The Ebb-Tide* is a story about the white man in the tropics, and it is grim if not, as Stevenson asserted, in its portrayal of character, at least in its assessment of the moral reality of that encounter.

DAVID DAICHES

NOTE ON THE TEXT

The Ebb-Tide was first published as a serial in *To-Day* between November 1893 and February 1894. It first appeared in book form in the United States in July 1894 and in Britain in September 1894 under the title 'The Ebb-Tide: *A Trio and Quartette*.' This edition uses the 1894 text with small changes to modernise spelling and punctuation.

THE EBB-TIDE
A Trio and Quartette
'There is a tide in the affairs of men.'

NOTE

On the pronunciation of a name very
frequently repeated on these pages, the
reader may take for a guide:

"It was the schooner *Farallone*."

R. L. S.
L. O.

NOTE

by Lloyd Osbourne

Stevenson and I little knew, when we began our collaboration, that we were afterwards to raise such a hornets' nest about our ears. The critics resented such an unequal partnership, and made it impossible for us to continue it. It may be that they were right; they wanted Stevenson's best, and felt pretty sure they would not get it in our collaboration. But when they ascribed all the good in our three books to Stevenson and all the bad to me, they went a little beyond the mark. It is a pleasure to me to recall that the early part of both *The Wrecker* and *The Ebb-Tide* was almost entirely my own; so also were the storm scenes of the *Norah Creina*; so also the fight on the *Flying Scud*; so also the inception of Huish's scheme, the revelation of it to his companions, his landing on the atoll with the bottle of vitriol in his breast. On the other hand, the Paris portion of *The Wrecker* was all Stevenson's, as well as the concluding chapters of both the South Sea books.

It is not possible to disentangle anything else that was wholly mine or his – the blending was too complete, our method of work too criss-crossed and intimate. For instance, we would begin by outlining the story in a general way; this done, we marshalled it into chapters, with a few explanatory words to each; then it was time for me to write the first draft of Chapter 1. This I would read to him, and if it were satisfactory it was laid to one side; but if it were not, I would rewrite it, embodying his criticisms. Each chapter in turn was fully discussed in advance before I put pen to paper; and in this way, though the actual first draft was in my own hand, the form of the story continually took shape under Stevenson's eyes. When my first draft of the entire book was finished he would rewrite it again from cover to cover.

I can remember nothing more delightful than the days we thus passed together. If our three books are in no wise great, they preserve, it seems to me, something of the zest and exhilaration that went into their making – the good humour, the eagerness.

We were both under the glamour of the Islands – and that life, so strange, so picturesque, so animated, took us both by storm. Kings and beachcombers, pearl-fishers and princesses, traders, slavers, and schooner-captains, castaways, and runaways – what a world it was! And all this in a fairyland of palms, and glassy bays, and little lost settlements nestling at the foot of forest and mountain, with kings to make brotherhood with us, and a dubious white man or two, in earrings and pyjamas, no less insistent to extend to us the courtesies of the "beach."

It was amid such people, and amid such scenes, that *The Ebb-Tide* and *The Wrecker* were written.

Part I
THE TRIO

Chapter 1

NIGHT ON THE BEACH

Throughout the island world of the Pacific, scattered men of many European races and from almost every grade of society carry activity and disseminate disease. Some prosper, some vegetate. Some have mounted the steps of thrones and owned islands and navies. Others again must marry for a livelihood; a strapping, merry, chocolate-coloured dame supports them in sheer idleness; and, dressed like natives, but still retaining some foreign element of gait or attitude, still perhaps with some relic (such as a single eye-glass) of the officer and gentleman, they sprawl in palm-leaf verandahs and entertain an island audience with memoirs of the music-hall. And there are still others, less pliable, less capable, less fortunate, perhaps less base, who continue, even in these isles of plenty, to lack bread.

At the far end of the town of Papeete, three such men were seated on the beach under a *purao* tree.

It was late. Long ago the band had broken up and marched musically home, a motley troop of men and women, merchant clerks and navy officers, dancing in its wake, arms about waist and crowned with garlands. Long ago darkness and silence had gone from house to house about the tiny pagan city. Only the street lamps shone on, making a glow-worm halo in the umbrageous alleys or drawing a tremulous image on the waters of the port. A sound of snoring ran among the piles of lumber by the Government pier. It was wafted ashore from the graceful clipper-bottomed schooners, where they lay moored close in like dinghies, and their crews were stretched upon the deck under the open sky or huddled in a rude tent amidst the disorder of merchandise.

But the men under the *purao* had no thought of sleep. The same temperature in England would have passed without remark in summer; but it was bitter cold for the South Seas. Inanimate nature knew it, and the bottle of cocoanut oil stood frozen in every bird-cage house about the island; and the men knew it, and shivered. They wore flimsy cotton clothes, the same they had sweated in by day and run the gauntlet of the tropic showers; and to complete their evil case, they had no breakfast to mention, less dinner, and no supper at all.

In the telling South Sea phrase, these three men were *on the beach*. Common calamity had brought them acquainted, as the three most miserable English-speaking creatures in Tahiti; and beyond their misery, they knew next to nothing of each other, not even their true names. For each had made a long apprenticeship in going downward; and each, at some stage of the descent, had been shamed into the adoption of an *alias*. And yet not one of them had figured in a court of justice; two were men of kindly virtues; and one, as he sat and shivered under the *purao*, had a tattered Virgil in his pocket.

Certainly, if money could have been raised upon the book, Robert Herrick would long ago have sacrificed that last possession; but the demand for literature, which is so marked a feature in some parts of the South Seas, extends not so far as the dead tongues; and the Virgil, which he could not exchange against a meal, had often consoled him in his hunger. He would study it, as he lay with tightened belt on the floor of the old calaboose, seeking favourite passages and finding new ones only less beautiful because they lacked the consecration of remembrance. Or he would pause on random country walks; sit on the path side, gazing over the sea on the mountains of Eimeo;* and dip into the *Aeneid*, seeking *sortes*.* And if the oracle (as is the way of oracles) replied with no very certain nor encouraging voice, visions of England at least would throng upon the exile's memory: the busy schoolroom, the green playing-fields, holidays at home, and the perennial roar of London, and the fireside, and the white head of his father. For it is the destiny of those grave, restrained and classic writers, with whom we make enforced and often painful acquaintanceship at school, to pass into the blood and become native in the memory; so that a phrase of

Virgil speaks not so much of Mantua or Augustus, but of English places and the student's own irrevocable youth.

Robert Herrick was the son of an intelligent, active, and ambitious man, small partner in a considerable London house. Hopes were conceived of the boy; he was sent to a good school, gained there an Oxford scholarship, and proceeded in course to the Western University. With all his talent and taste (and he had much of both) Robert was deficient in consistency and intellectual manhood, wandered in bypaths of study, worked at music or at metaphysics when he should have been at Greek, and took at last a paltry degree. Almost at the same time, the London house was disastrously wound up; Mr Herrick must begin the world again as a clerk in a strange office, and Robert relinquish his ambitions and accept with gratitude a career that he detested and despised. He had no head for figures, no interest in affairs, detested the constraint of hours, and despised the aims and the success of merchants. To grow rich was none of his ambitions; rather to do well. A worse or a more bold young man would have refused the destiny; perhaps tried his future with his pen; perhaps enlisted. Robert, more prudent, possibly more timid, consented to embrace that way of life in which he could most readily assist his family. But he did so with a mind divided; fled the neighbourhood of former comrades; and chose, out of several positions placed at his disposal, a clerkship in New York.

His career thenceforth was one of unbroken shame. He did not drink, he was exactly honest, he was never rude to his employers, yet was everywhere discharged. Bringing no interest to his duties, he brought no attention; his day was a tissue of things neglected and things done amiss; and from place to place and from town to town, he carried the character of one thoroughly incompetent. No man can bear the word applied to him without some flush of colour, as indeed there is none other that so emphatically slams in a man's face the door of self-respect. And to Herrick, who was conscious of talents and acquirements, who looked down upon those humble duties in which he was found wanting, the pain was the more exquisite. Early in his fall, he had ceased to be able to make remittances;

shortly after, having nothing but failure to communicate, he ceased writing home; and about a year before this tale begins, turned suddenly upon the streets of San Francisco by a vulgar and infuriated German Jew, he had broken the last bonds of self-respect, and upon a sudden impulse, changed his name and invested his last dollar in a passage on the mail brigantine, the *City of Papeete*. With what expectation he had trimmed his flight for the South Seas, Herrick perhaps scarcely knew. Doubtless there were fortunes to be made in pearl and copra; doubtless others not more gifted than himself had climbed in the island world to be queen's consorts and king's ministers. But if Herrick had gone there with any manful purpose, he would have kept his father's name; the *alias* betrayed his moral bankruptcy; he had struck his flag; he entertained no hope to reinstate himself or help his straitened family; and he came to the islands (where he knew the climate to be soft, bread cheap, and manners easy) a skulker from life's battle and his own immediate duty. Failure, he had said, was his portion; let it be a pleasant failure.

It is fortunately not enough to say 'I will be base.' Herrick continued in the islands his career of failure; but in the new scene and under the new name, he suffered no less sharply than before. A place was got, it was lost in the old style; from the long-suffering of the keepers of restaurants he fell to more open charity upon the wayside; as time went on, good nature became weary, and after a repulse or two, Herrick became shy. There were women enough who would have supported a far worse and a far uglier man; Herrick never met or never knew them: or if he did both, some manlier feeling would revolt, and he preferred starvation. Drenched with rains, broiling by day, shivering by night, a disused and ruinous prison for a bedroom, his diet begged or pilfered out of rubbish heaps, his associates two creatures equally outcast with himself, he had drained for months the cup of penitence. He had known what it was to be resigned, what it was to break forth in a childish fury of rebellion against fate, and what it was to sink into the coma of despair. The time had changed him. He told himself no longer tales of an easy and perhaps agreeable declension; he read his nature otherwise; he had proved himself incapable of rising, and he now learned by experience that he could not stoop to fall. Something that was scarcely pride or strength, that was perhaps only refinement, withheld him from capitulation; but he looked on upon his own misfortune with a growing rage, and sometimes wondered at his patience.

It was now the fourth month completed, and still there was no change or sign of change. The moon, racing through a world of flying clouds of every size and shape and density, some black as ink stains, some delicate as lawn, threw the marvel of her Southern brightness over the same lovely and detested scene: the island mountains crowned with the perennial island cloud, the embowered city studded with rare lamps, the masts in the harbour, the smooth mirror of the lagoon, and the mole of the barrier reef on which the breakers whitened. The moon shone too, with bull's-eye sweeps, on his companions; on the stalwart frame of the American who called himself Brown, and was known to be a master mariner in some disgrace; and on the dwarfish person, the pale eyes and toothless smile of a vulgar and bad-hearted cockney clerk. Here was society for Robert Herrick! The Yankee skipper was a man at least: he had sterling qualities of tenderness and resolution; he was one whose hand you could take without a blush. But there was no redeeming grace about the other, who called himself sometimes Hay and sometimes Tomkins, and laughed at the discrepancy; who had been employed in every store in Papeete, for the creature was able in his way; who had been discharged from each in turn, for he was wholly vile; who had alienated all his old employers so that they passed him in the street as if he were a dog, and all his old comrades so that they shunned him as they would a creditor.

Not long before, a ship from Peru had brought an influenza, and it now raged in the island, and particularly in Papeete. From all round the *purao* arose and fell a dismal sound of men coughing, and strangling as they coughed. The sick natives, with the islander's impatience of a touch of fever, had crawled from their houses to be cool and, squatting on the shore or on the beached canoes, painfully expected the new day. Even as the crowing of cocks goes about the country in the night from farm to farm, accesses of coughing arose, and spread, and died in the distance, and sprang up again. Each miserable shiverer caught the suggestion from his neighbour, was torn for some minutes by that cruel ecstasy, and left spent and without voice or courage when it passed. If a man had pity to spend, Papeete beach, in that cold night and in that infected season, was a place to spend it on. And of all the sufferers, perhaps the least deserving, but surely the most pitiable, was the London clerk. He was used to another life, to houses, beds, nursing, and the dainties of the sickroom; he lay there now, in the cold open, exposed to the gusting of the wind, and with an empty belly. He was besides infirm; the disease shook him to the vitals; and his companions watched his endurance with surprise. A profound commiseration filled them, and contended with and conquered their abhorrence. The disgust attendant on so ugly a sickness magnified this dislike; at the same time, and with more than compensating strength, shame for a sentiment so inhuman bound them the more straitly to his service; and even the evil they knew of him swelled their solicitude, for the thought of death is always the least supportable when it draws near to the merely sensual and selfish. Sometimes they held him up; sometimes, with mistaken helpfulness, they beat him between the shoulders; and when the poor wretch lay back ghastly and spent after a paroxysm of coughing, they would sometimes peer into his face, doubtfully exploring it for any mark of life. There is no one but has some virtue: that of the clerk was courage; and he would make haste to reassure them in a pleasantry not always decent.

'I'm all right, pals,' he gasped once: 'this is the thing to strengthen the muscles of the larynx.'

'Well, you take the cake!' cried the captain.

'O, I'm good plucked enough,' pursued the sufferer with a broken utterance. 'But it do seem bloomin' hard to me, that I should be the only party down with this form of vice, and the only one to do the funny business. I think one of you other parties might wake up. Tell a fellow something.'

'The trouble is we've nothing to tell, my son,' returned the captain.

'I'll tell you, if you like, what I was thinking,' said Herrick.

'Tell us anything,' said the clerk, 'I only want to be reminded that I ain't dead.'

Herrick took up his parable, lying on his face and speaking slowly and scarce above his breath, not like a man who has anything to say, but like one talking against time.

'Well, I was thinking this,' he began: 'I was thinking I lay on Papeete beach one night – all moon and squalls and fellows coughing – and I was cold and hungry, and down in the mouth, and was about ninety years of age, and had spent two hundred and twenty of them on Papeete beach. And I was thinking I wished I had a ring to rub, or had a fairy godmother, or could raise Beelzebub. And I was trying to remember how you did it. I knew you made a ring of skulls, for I had seen that in the *Freischütz*:* and that you took off your coat and turned up your sleeves, for I had seen Formes do that when he was playing Kaspar,* and you could see (by the way he went about it) it was a business he had studied; and that you ought to have something to kick up a smoke and a bad smell, I dare say a cigar might do, and that you ought to say the Lord's Prayer backwards. Well, I wondered if I could do that; it seemed rather a feat, you see. And then I wondered if I would say it forward, and I thought I did. Well, no sooner had I got to *world without end*, than I saw a man in a *pariu*, and with a mat under his arm, come along the beach from the town. He was rather a hard-favoured old party, and he limped and crippled, and all the time he kept coughing. At first I didn't cotton to his looks, I thought, and then I got sorry for the old soul because he coughed so hard. I remembered that we had some of that cough mixture the American consul gave the captain for Hay. It never did Hay a ha'porth of service, but I thought it might do the old gentleman's business for him, and stood up. "*Yorana!*" says I. "*Yorana!*" says he. "Look here," I said, "I've got some first-rate stuff in a bottle; it'll fix your cough, savvy? *Harry my*[1]

[1] Come here.

and I'll measure you a tablespoonful in the palm of my hand, for all our plate is at the bankers." So I thought the old party came up, and the nearer he came, the less I took to him. But I had passed my word, you see.'

'Wot is this bloomin' drivel?' interrupted the clerk. 'It's like the rot there is in tracts.'

'It's a story; I used to tell them to the kids at home,' said Herrick. 'If it bores you, I'll drop it.'

'O, cut along!' returned the sick man, irritably. 'It's better than nothing.'

'Well,' continued Herrick, 'I had no sooner given him the cough mixture than he seemed to straighten up and change, and I saw he wasn't a Tahitian after all, but some kind of Arab, and had a long beard on his chin. "One good turn deserves another," says he. "I am a magician out of the *Arabian Nights*, and this mat that I have under my arm is the original carpet of Mohammed Ben Somebody-or-other. Say the word, and you can have a cruise upon the carpet." "You don't mean to say this is the Travelling Carpet?" I cried. "You bet I do," said he. "You've been to America since last I read the *Arabian Nights*," said I, a little suspicious. "I should think so," said he. "Been everywhere. A man with a carpet like this isn't going to moulder in a semi-detached villa." Well, that struck me as reasonable. "All right," I said; "and do you mean to tell me I can get on that carpet and go straight to London, England?" I said, "London, England," captain, because he seemed to have been so long in your part of the world. "In the crack of a whip," said he. I figured up the time. What is the difference between Papeete and London, captain?'

'Taking Greenwich and Point Venus,* nine hours, odd minutes and seconds,' replied the mariner.

'Well, that's about what I made it,' resumed Herrick, 'about nine hours. Calling this three in the morning, I made out I would drop into London about noon; and the idea tickled me immensely. "There's only one bother," I said, "I haven't a copper cent. It would be a pity to go to London and not buy the morning *Standard*." "O!" said he, "you don't realise the conveniences of this carpet. You see this pocket? you've only got to stick your hand in, and you pull it out filled with sovereigns."'

'Double-eagles, wasn't it?' inquired the captain.

'That was what it was!' cried Herrick. 'I thought they seemed unusually big, and I remember now I had to go to the money-changers at Charing Cross and get English silver.'

'O, you went there?' said the clerk. 'Wot did you do? Bet you had a B. and S.!'*

'Well, you see, it was just as the old boy said – like the cut of a whip,' said Herrick. 'The one minute I was here on the beach at three in the morning, the next I was in front of the Golden Cross at midday. At first I was dazzled, and covered my eyes, and there didn't seem the smallest change; the roar of the Strand and the roar of the reef were like the same: hark to it now, and you can hear the cabs and buses rolling and the streets resound! And then at last I could look about, and there was the old place, and no mistake! With the statues in the square, and St Martin's-in-the-Fields, and the bobbies, and the sparrows, and the hacks; and I can't tell you what I felt like. I felt like crying, I believe, or dancing, or jumping clean over the Nelson Column. I was like a fellow caught up out of Hell and flung down into the dandiest part of Heaven. Then I spotted for a hansom with a spanking horse. "A shilling for yourself, if you're there in twenty minutes!" said I to the jarvey.* He went a good pace, though of course it was a trifle to the carpet; and in nineteen minutes and a half I was at the door.'

'What door?' asked the captain.

'Oh, a house I know of,' returned Herrick.

'But it was a public-house!' cried the clerk – only these were not his words. 'And w'y didn't you take the carpet there instead of trundling in a growler?'*

'I didn't want to startle a quiet street,' said the narrator. 'Bad form. And besides, it was a hansom.'

'Well, and what did you do next?' inquired the captain.

'Oh, I went in,' said Herrick.

'The old folks?' asked the captain.

'That's about it,' said the other, chewing a grass.

'Well, I think you are about the poorest 'and at a yarn!' cried the clerk. 'Crikey, it's like *Ministering Children*! I can tell you there would be more beer and skittles about my little jaunt. I would go and have a B. and S. for luck. Then I would get a big ulster* with astrakhan fur, and take my cane and do the la-de-la down Piccadilly. Then I would go to a slap-up restaurant, and have green peas, and a bottle of fizz, and a chump chop – Oh! and I forgot, I'd 'ave some devilled whitebait first – and green gooseberry tart, and 'ot coffee, and some of that form of vice in big bottles with a seal – Benedictine – that's the bloomin' nyme! Then I'd drop into a theatre, and pal on with some chappies, and do the dancing rooms and bars, and that, and wouldn't go 'ome till morning, till daylight doth appear. And the next day I'd have water-cresses, 'am, muffin, and fresh butter; wouldn't I just, O my!'

The clerk was interrupted by a fresh attack of coughing.

'Well, now, I'll tell you what I would do,' said the captain: 'I would have none of your fancy rigs with the man driving from the mizzen cross-trees, but a plain fore-and-aft hack cab of the highest registered tonnage. First of all, I would bring up at the market and get a turkey and a sucking-pig. Then I'd go to a wine merchant's and get a dozen of champagne, and a dozen of some sweet wine, rich and sticky and strong, something in the port or madeira line, the best in the store. Then I'd bear up for a toy-store, and lay out twenty dollars in assorted toys for the piccaninnies; and then to a confectioner's and take in cakes and pies and fancy bread, and that stuff with the plums in it; and then to a news-agency and buy all the papers, all the picture ones for the kids, and all the story papers for the old girl about the Earl discovering himself to Anna-Mariar and the escape of the Lady Maude from the private madhouse; and then I'd tell the fellow to drive home.'

'There ought to be some syrup for the kids,' suggested Herrick; 'they like syrup.'

'Yes, syrup for the kids, red syrup at that!' said the captain. 'And those things they pull at, and go pop, and have measly poetry inside. And then I tell you we'd have a thanksgiving day and Christmas tree combined. Great Scott, but I would like to see the kids! I guess they would light right out of the house, when they saw daddy driving up. My little Adar—'

The captain stopped sharply.

'Well, keep it up!' said the clerk.

'The damned thing is, I don't know if they ain't starving!' cried the captain.

'They can't be worse off than we are, and that's one comfort,' returned the clerk. 'I defy the devil to make me worse off.'

It seemed as if the devil heard him. The light of the moon had been some time cut off and they had talked in darkness. Now there was heard a roar, which drew impetuously nearer; the face of the lagoon was seen to whiten; and before they had staggered to their feet, a squall burst in rain upon the outcasts. The rage and volume of that avalanche one must have lived in the tropics to conceive; a man panted in its assault, as he might pant under a shower-bath; and the world seemed whelmed in night and water.

They fled, groping for their usual shelter – it might be almost called their home – in the old calaboose; came drenched into its empty chambers; and lay down, three sops of humanity on the cold coral floors, and presently, when the squall was overpast, the others could hear in the darkness the chattering of the clerk's teeth.

'I say, you fellows,' he wailed, 'for God's sake, lie up and try to warm me. I'm blymed if I don't think I'll die else!'

So the three crept together into one wet mass, and lay until day came, shivering and dozing off, and continually re-awakened to wretchedness by the coughing of the clerk.

Chapter 2

MORNING ON THE BEACH —
THE THREE LETTERS

The clouds were all fled, the beauty of the tropic day was spread
upon Papeete; and the wall of breaking seas upon the reef, and
the palms upon the islet, already trembled in the heat. A French
man-of-war was going out, homeward bound; she lay in the
middle distance of the port, an ant heap for activity. In the night
a schooner had come in, and now lay far out, hard by the
passage; and the yellow flag, the emblem of pestilence, flew on
her. From up the coast, a long procession of canoes headed
round the point and towards the market, bright as a scarf with
the many-coloured clothing of the natives and the piles of fruit.
But not even the beauty and the welcome warmth of the
morning, not even these naval movements, so interesting to
sailors and to idlers, could engage the attention of the outcasts.
They were still cold at heart, their mouths sour from the want
of sleep, their steps rambling from the lack of food; and they
strung like lame geese along the beach in a disheartened silence.
It was towards the town they moved; towards the town whence
smoke arose, where happier folk were breakfasting; and as they
went, their hungry eyes were upon all sides, but they were only
scouting for a meal.

A small and dingy schooner lay snug against the quay, with
which it was connected by a plank. On the forward deck, under
a spot of awning, five Kanakas who made up the crew, were
squatted round a basin of fried feis,[1] and drinking coffee from
tin mugs.

'Eight bells: knock off for breakfast!' cried the captain with a

---

[1] *Fei* is the hill banana.

miserable heartiness. 'Never tried this craft before; positively my first appearance; guess I'll draw a bumper house.'

He came close up to where the plank rested on the grassy quay; turned his back upon the schooner, and began to whistle that lively air, 'The Irish Washerwoman.' It caught the ears of the Kanaka seamen like a preconcerted signal; with one accord they looked up from their meal and crowded to the ship's side, fei in hand and munching as they looked. Even as a poor brown Pyrenean bear dances in the streets of English towns under his master's baton; even so, but with how much more of spirit and precision, the captain footed it in time to his own whistling, and his long morning shadow capered beyond him on the grass. The Kanakas smiled on the performance; Herrick looked on heavy-eyed, hunger for the moment conquering all sense of shame; and a little farther off, but still hard by, the clerk was torn by the seven devils of the influenza.

The captain stopped suddenly, appeared to perceive his audience for the first time, and represented the part of a man surprised in his private hour of pleasure.

'Hello!' said he.

The Kanakas clapped hands and called upon him to go on.

'No, *sir*!' said the captain. 'No eat, no dance. Savvy?'

'Poor old man!' returned one of the crew. 'Him no eat?'

'Lord, no!' said the captain. 'Like-um too much eat. No got.'

'All right. Me got,' said the sailor; 'you tome here. Plenty toffee, plenty fei. Nutha man him tome too.'

'I guess we'll drop right in,' observed the captain; and he and his companions hastened up the plank. They were welcomed on board with the shaking of hands; place was made for them about the basin; a sticky demijohn of molasses was added to the feast in honour of company, and an accordion brought from the forecastle and significantly laid by the performer's side.

'*Ariana*,'[1] said he lightly, touching the instrument as he spoke; and he fell to on a long savoury fei, made an end of it, raised his mug of coffee, and nodded across at the spokesman of the crew.

[1] By-and-bye.

'Here's your health, old man; you're a credit to the South Pacific,' said he.

With the unsightly greed of hounds they glutted themselves with the hot food and coffee; and even the clerk revived and the colour deepened in his eyes. The kettle was drained, the basin cleaned; their entertainers, who had waited on their wants throughout with the pleased hospitality of Polynesians, made haste to bring forward a dessert of island tobacco and rolls of pandanus leaf to serve as paper; and presently all sat about the dishes puffing like Indian Sachems.*

'When a man 'as breakfast every day, he don't know what it is,' observed the clerk.

'The next point is dinner,' said Herrick; and then with a passionate utterance: 'I wish to God I was a Kanaka!'

'There's one thing sure,' said the captain. 'I'm about desperate, I'd rather hang than rot here much longer.' And with the word he took the accordion and struck up. 'Home, sweet home.'

'O, drop that!' cried Herrick, 'I can't stand that.'

'No more can I,' said the captain. 'I've got to play something though: got to pay the shot, my son.' And he struck up 'John Brown's Body' in a fine sweet baritone: 'Dandy Jim of Carolina,' came next; 'Rorin the Bold,' 'Swing low, Sweet Chariot,' and 'The Beautiful Land' followed. The captain was paying his shot with usury, as he had done many a time before; many a meal had he bought with the same currency from the melodious-minded natives, always, as now, to their delight.

He was in the middle of 'Fifteen Dollars in the Inside Pocket,' singing with dogged energy, for the task went sore against the grain, when a sensation was suddenly to be observed among the crew.

'*Tapena Tom harry my*,'[1] said the spokesman, pointing.

And the three beachcombers, following his indication, saw the figure of a man in pyjama trousers and a white jumper approaching briskly from the town.

---

[1] 'Captain Tom is coming.'

'That's Tapena Tom, is it?' said the captain, pausing in his music. 'I don't seem to place the brute.'

'We'd better cut,' said the clerk. ''E's no good.'

'Well,' said the musician deliberately, 'one can't most generally always tell. I'll try it on, I guess. Music has charms to soothe the savage Tapena, boys. We might strike it rich; it might amount to iced punch in the cabin.'

'Hiced punch? O my!' said the clerk. 'Give him something 'ot, captain. "Way down the Swannee River"; try that.'

'No, *sir*! Looks Scotch,' said the captain; and he struck, for his life, into 'Auld Lang Syne.'

Captain Tom continued to approach with the same businesslike alacrity; no change was to be perceived in his bearded face as he came swinging up the plank: he did not even turn his eyes on the performer.

> 'We twa hae paidled in the burn
> Frae morning tide till dine,'*

went the song.

Captain Tom had a parcel under his arm, which he laid on the house roof, and then turning suddenly to the strangers: 'Here, you!' he bellowed, 'be off out of that!'

The clerk and Herrick stood not on the order of their going, but fled incontinently by the plank. The performer, on the other hand, flung down the instrument and rose to his full height slowly.

'What's that you say?' he said. 'I've half a mind to give you a lesson in civility.'

'You set up any more of your gab to me,' returned the Scotsman, 'and I'll show ye the wrong side of a jyle. I've heard tell of the three of ye. Ye're not long for here, I can tell ye that. The Government has their eyes upon ye. They make short work of damned beachcombers, I'll say that for the French.'

'You wait till I catch you off your ship!' cried the captain: and then, turning to the crew, 'Good-bye, you fellows!' he said. 'You're gentlemen, anyway! The worst nigger among you would look better upon a quarter-deck than that filthy Scotchman.'

Captain Tom scorned to reply; he watched with a hard smile the departure of his guests; and as soon as the last foot was off the plank; turned to the hands to work cargo.

The beachcombers beat their inglorious retreat along the shore; Herrick first, his face dark with blood, his knees trembling under him with the hysteria of rage. Presently, under the same *purao* where they had shivered the night before, he cast himself down, and groaned aloud, and ground his face into the sand.

'Don't speak to me, don't speak to me. I can't stand it,' broke from him.

The other two stood over him perplexed.

'Wot can't he stand now?' said the clerk. ''Asn't he 'ad a meal? *I'm* lickin' my lips.'

Herrick reared up his wild eyes and burning face. 'I can't beg!' he screamed, and again threw himself prone.

'This thing's got to come to an end,' said the captain with an intake of the breath.

'Looks like signs of an end, don't it?' sneered the clerk.

'He's not so far from it, and don't you deceive yourself,' replied the captain. 'Well,' he added in a livelier voice, 'you fellows hang on here, and I'll go and interview my representative.'

Whereupon he turned on his heel, and set off at a swinging sailor's walk towards Papeete.

It was some half hour later when he returned. The clerk was dozing with his back against the tree: Herrick still lay where he had flung himself; nothing showed whether he slept or waked.

'See, boys!' cried the captain, with that artificial heartiness of his which was at times so painful, 'here's a new idea.' And he produced note paper, stamped envelopes, and pencils, three of each. 'We can all write home by the mail brigantine; the consul says I can come over to his place and ink up the addresses.'

'Well, that's a start, too,' said the clerk. 'I never thought of that.'

'It was that yarning last night about going home that put me up to it,' said the captain.

'Well, 'and over,' said the clerk. 'I'll 'ave a shy,' and he retired a little distance to the shade of a canoe.

The others remained under the *purao*. Now they would write a word or two, now scribble it out; now they would sit biting at the pencil end and staring seaward; now their eyes would rest on the clerk, where he sat propped on the canoe, leering and coughing, his pencil racing glibly on the paper.

'I can't do it,' said Herrick suddenly. 'I haven't got the heart.'

'See here,' said the captain, speaking with unwonted gravity; 'it may be hard to write, and to write lies at that; and God knows it is; but it's the square thing. It don't cost anything to say you're well and happy, and sorry you can't make a remittance this mail; and if you don't, I'll tell you what I think it is – I think it's about the high-water mark of being a brute beast.'

'It's easy to talk,' said Herrick. 'You don't seem to have written much yourself, I notice.'

'What do you bring in me for?' broke from the captain. His voice was indeed scarce raised above a whisper, but emotion clanged in it. 'What do you know about me? If you had commanded the finest barque that ever sailed from Portland;* if you had been drunk in your berth when she struck the breakers in Fourteen Island Group, and hadn't had the wit to stay there and drown, but came on deck, and given drunken orders, and lost six lives – I could understand your talking then! There,' he said more quietly, 'that's my yarn, and now you know it. It's a pretty one for the father of a family. Five men and a woman murdered. Yes, there was a woman on board, and hadn't no business to be either. Guess I sent her to Hell, if there is such a place. I never dared go home again; and the wife and the little ones went to England to her father's place. I don't know what's come to them,' he added, with a bitter shrug.

'Thank you, captain,' said Herrick. 'I never liked you better.'

They shook hands, short and hard, with eyes averted, tenderness swelling in their bosoms.

'Now, boys! to work again at lying!' said the captain.

'I'll give my father up,' returned Herrick with a writhen smile. 'I'll try my sweetheart instead for a change of evils.'

And here is what he wrote:

'Emma, I have scratched out the beginning to my father, for I think I can write more easily to you. This is my last farewell to all, the last you will ever hear or see of an unworthy friend and son. I have failed in life; I am quite broken down and disgraced. I pass under a false name; you will have to tell my father that with all your kindness. It is my own fault. I know, had I chosen, that I might have done well; and yet I swear to you I tried to choose. I could not bear that you should think I did not try. For I loved you all; you must never doubt me in that, you least of all. I have always unceasingly loved, but what was my love worth? and what was I worth? I had not the manhood of a common clerk, I could not work to earn you; I have lost you now, and for your sake I could be glad of it. When you first came to my father's house – do you remember those days? I want you to – you saw the best of me then, all that was good in me. Do you remember the day I took your hand and would not let it go – and the day on Battersea Bridge, when we were looking at a barge, and I began to tell you one of my silly stories, and broke off to say I loved you? That was the beginning, and now here is the end. When you have read this letter, you will go round and kiss them all good-bye, my father and mother, and the children, one by one, and poor uncle; and tell them all to forget me, and forget me yourself. Turn the key in the door; let no thought of me return; be done with the poor ghost that pretended he was a man and stole your love. Scorn of myself grinds in me as I write. I should tell you I am well and happy, and want for nothing. I do not exactly make money, or I should send a remittance; but I am well cared for, have friends, live in a beautiful place and climate, such as we have dreamed of together, and no pity need be wasted on me. In such places, you understand, it is easy to live, and live well, but often hard to make sixpence in money. Explain this to my father, he will understand. I have no more to say; only linger, going out, like an unwilling guest. God in heaven bless you. Think of me to the last, here, on a bright beach, the sky and sea immoderately blue, and the great breakers roaring outside on a barrier reef, where a little isle sits green with palms. I am well and strong. It is a more pleasant way to die than if you were crowding about me on a sick-bed. And yet I am dying. This is my last kiss. Forgive, forget the unworthy.'

So far he had written, his paper was all filled, when there returned a memory of evenings at the piano, and that song, the masterpiece of love, in which so many have found the expression of their dearest thoughts. '*Einst, O wunder!*'* he added. More was not required; he knew that in his love's heart the context would spring up, escorted with fair images and harmony; of how all through life her name should tremble in his ears, her name be everywhere repeated in the sounds of nature; and when death came, and he lay dissolved, her memory lingered and thrilled among his elements.

> 'Once, O wonder! once from the ashes of my heart
> Arose a blossom—'

Herrick and the captain finished their letters about the same time; each was breathing deep, and their eyes met and were averted as they closed the envelopes.

'Sorry I write so big,' said the captain gruffly. 'Came all of a rush, when it did come.'

'Same here,' said Herrick. 'I could have done with a ream when I got started; but it's long enough for all the good I had to say.'

They were still at the addresses when the clerk strolled up, smirking and twirling his envelope, like a man well pleased. He looked over Herrick's shoulder.

'Hullo,' he said, 'you ain't writing 'ome.'

'I am, though,' said Herrick; 'she lives with my father. Oh, I see what you mean,' he added. 'My real name is Herrick. No more Hay' – they had both used the same *alias* – 'no more Hay than yours, I dare say.'

'Clean bowled in the middle stump!' laughed the clerk. 'My name's 'Uish if you want to know. Everybody has a false nyme in the Pacific. Lay you five to three the captain 'as.'

'So I have too,' replied the captain; 'and I've never told my own since the day I tore the title page out of my Bowditch and flung the damned thing into the sea. But I'll tell it to you, boys. John Davis is my name. I'm Davis of the *Sea Ranger*.'

'Dooce you are!' said Hush. 'And what was she? a pirate or a slyver?'

'She was the fastest barque out of Portland, Maine,' replied the captain; 'and for the way I lost her, I might as well have bored a hole in her side with an auger.'

'Oh, you lost her, did you?' said the clerk. ''Ope she was insured?'

No answer being returned to this sally, Huish, still brimming over with vanity and conversation, struck into another subject.

'I've a good mind to read you my letter,' said he. 'I've a good fist with a pen when I choose, and this is a prime lark. She was a barmaid I ran across in Northampton; she was a spanking fine piece, no end of style; and we cottoned at first sight like parties in the play. I suppose I spent the chynge of a fiver on that girl. Well, I 'appened to remember her nyme, so I wrote to her, and told her 'ow I had got rich, and married a queen in the Hislands, and lived in a blooming palace. Such a sight of crammers! I must read you one bit about my opening the nigger parliament in a cocked 'at. It's really prime.'

The captain jumped to his feet. 'That's what you did with the paper that I went and begged for you?' he roared.

It was perhaps lucky for Huish – it was surely in the end unfortunate for all – that he was seized just then by one of his prostrating accesses of cough; his comrades would have else deserted him, so bitter was their resentment. When the fit had passed, the clerk reached out his hand, picked up the letter, which had fallen to the earth, and tore it into fragments, stamp and all.

'Does that satisfy you?' he asked sullenly.

'We'll say no more about it,' replied Davis.

Chapter 3

THE OLD CALABOOSE —
DESTINY AT THE DOOR

The old calaboose, in which the waifs had so long harboured, is a low, rectangular enclosure of building at the corner of a shady western avenue and a little townward of the British consulate. Within was a grassy court, littered with wreckage and the traces of vagrant occupation. Six or seven cells opened from the court: the doors, that had once been locked on mutinous whalermen, rotting before them in the grass. No mark remained of their old destination, except the rusty bars upon the windows.

The floor of one of the cells had been a little cleared; a bucket (the last remaining piece of furniture of the three caitiffs) stood full of water by the door, a half cocoanut shell beside it for a drinking cup; and on some ragged ends of mat Huish sprawled asleep, his mouth open, his face deathly. The glow of the tropic afternoon, the green of sunbright foliage, stared into that shady place through door and window; and Herrick, pacing to and fro on the coral floor, sometimes paused and laved his face and neck with tepid water from the bucket. His long arrears of suffering, the night's vigil, the insults of the morning, and the harrowing business of the letter, had strung him to that point when pain is almost pleasure, time shrinks to a mere point, and death and life appear indifferent. To and fro he paced like a caged brute; his mind whirling through the universe of thought and memory; his eyes, as he went, skimming the legends on the wall. The crumbling whitewash was all full of them: Tahitian names, and French, and English, and rude sketches of ships under sail and men at fisticuffs.

It came to him of a sudden that he too must leave upon these walls the memorial of his passage. He paused before a clean space, took the pencil out, and pondered. Vanity, so hard to dislodge, awoke in him. We call it vanity at least; perhaps unjustly. Rather it was the bare sense of his existence prompted him; the sense of his life, the one thing wonderful, to which he scarce clung with a finger. From his jarred nerves there came a strong sentiment of coming change; whether good or ill he could not say: change, he knew no more – change, with inscrutable veiled face, approaching noiseless. With the feeling, came the vision of a concert room, the rich hues of instruments, the silent audience, and the loud voice of the symphony. 'Destiny knocking at the door,' he thought; drew a stave on the plaster, and wrote in the famous phrase from the Fifth Symphony.* 'So,' thought he, 'they will know that I loved music and had classical tastes. They? He, I suppose: the unknown, kindred spirit that shall come some day and read my *memor querela*.* Ha, he shall have Latin too!' And he added: *terque quaterque beati Queis ante ora patrum.**

He turned again to his uneasy pacing, but now with an irrational and supporting sense of duty done. He had dug his grave that morning; now he had carved his epitaph; the folds of the toga were composed, why should he delay the insignificant trifle that remained to do? He paused and looked long in the face of the sleeping Huish, drinking disenchantment and distaste of life. He nauseated himself with that vile countenance. Could the thing continue? What bound him now? Had he no rights? – only the obligation to go on, without discharge or furlough, bearing the unbearable? *Ich trage unerträgliches*,* the quotation rose in his mind; he repeated the whole piece, one of the most perfect of the most perfect of poets; and a phrase struck him like a blow: *Du, stolzes Herz, du hast es ja gewollt.* Where was the pride of his heart? And he raged against himself, as a man bites on a sore tooth, in a heady sensuality of scorn. 'I have no pride, I have no heart, no manhood,' he thought, 'or why should I prolong a life more shameful than the gallows? Or why should I have fallen to it? No pride, no capacity, no force. Not even a bandit! and to be starving here with worse than banditti – with this trivial hell-hound!' His rage against his comrade rose and flooded him, and he shook a trembling fist at the sleeper.

A swift step was audible. The captain appeared upon the threshold of the cell, panting and flushed, and with a foolish face of happiness. In his arms he carried a loaf of bread and bottles of beer; the pockets of his coat were bulging with cigars. He rolled his treasures on the floor, grasped Herrick by both hands, and crowed with laughter.

'Broach the beer!' he shouted. 'Broach the beer, and glory hallelujah!'

'Beer?' repeated Huish, struggling to his feet.

'Beer it is!' cried Davis. 'Beer and plenty of it. Any number of persons can use it (like Lyon's tooth-tablet) with perfect propriety and neatness. Who's to officiate?'

'Leave me alone for that,' said the clerk. He knocked the necks off with a lump of coral, and each drank in succession from the shell.

'Have a weed,' said Davis. 'It's all in the bill.'

'What is up?' asked Herrick.

The captain fell suddenly grave. 'I'm coming to that,' said he. 'I want to speak with Herrick here. You, Hay – or Huish, or whatever your name is – you take a weed and the other bottle, and go and see how the wind is down by the *purao*. I'll call you when you're wanted!'

'Hay? Secrets? That ain't the ticket,' said Huish.

'Look here, my son,' said the captain, 'this is business, and don't you make any mistake about it. If you're going to make trouble, you can have it your own way and stop right here. Only get the thing right: if Herrick and I go, we take the beer. Savvy?'

'Oh, I don't want to shove my oar in,' returned Huish. 'I'll cut right enough. Give me the swipes. You can jaw till you're blue in the face for what I care. I don't think it's the friendly touch: that's all.' And he shambled grumbling out of the cell into the staring sun.

The captain watched him clear of the courtyard; then turned to Herrick.

'What is it?' asked Herrick thickly.

'I'll tell you,' said Davis. 'I want to consult you. It's a chance we've got. What's that?' he cried, pointing to the music on the wall.

'What?' said the other. 'Oh, that! It's music; it's a phrase of Beethoven's I was writing up. It means Destiny knocking at the door.

'Does it?' said the captain, rather low; and he went near and studied the inscription; 'and this French?' he asked, pointing to the Latin.

'O, it just means I should have been luckier if I had died at home,' returned Herrick impatiently. 'What is this business?'

'Destiny knocking at the door,' repeated the captain; and then, looking over his shoulder. 'Well, Mr Herrick, that's about what it comes to,' he added.

'What do you mean? Explain yourself,' said Herrick.

But the captain was again staring at the music. 'About how long ago since you wrote up this truck?' he asked.

'What does it matter?' exclaimed Herrick. 'I dare say half an hour.'

'My God, it's strange!' cried Davis. 'There's some men would call that accidental: not me. That—' and he drew his thick finger under the music – 'that's what I call Providence.'

'You said we had a chance,' said Herrick.

'Yes, *sir*!' said the captain, wheeling suddenly face to face with his companion. 'I did so. If you're the man I take you for, we have a chance.'

'I don't know what you take me for,' was the reply. 'You can scarce take me too low.'

'Shake hands, Mr Herrick,' said the captain. 'I know you. You're a gentleman and a man of spirit. I didn't want to speak before that bummer there; you'll see why. But to you I'll rip it right out. I got a ship.'

'A ship?' cried Herrick. 'What ship?'

'That schooner we saw this morning off the passage.'

'The schooner with the hospital flag?'

'That's the hooker,' said Davis. 'She's the *Farallone*, hundred and sixty tons register, out of 'Frisco for Sydney, in California champagne. Captain, mate, and one hand all died of the smallpox, same as they had round in the Paumotus,* I guess. Captain and mate were the only white men; all the hands Kanakas; seems a queer kind of outfit from a Christian port. Three of them left and a cook; didn't know where they were; I can't think where they were either, if you come to that; Wiseman must have been on the booze, I guess, to sail the course he did. However, there *he* was, dead; and here are the Kanakas as good as lost. They bummed around at sea like the babes in the wood; and tumbled end-on upon Tahiti. The consul here took charge. He offered the berth to Williams; Williams had never had the smallpox and backed down. That was when I came in for the letter paper; I thought there was something up when the consul asked me to look in again; but I never let on to you fellows, so's you'd not be disappointed. Consul tried M'Neil; scared of smallpox. He tried Capirati, that Corsican and Leblue, or whatever his name is, wouldn't lay a hand on it; all too fond of their sweet lives. Last of all, when there wasn't nobody else left to offer it to, he offers it to me. "Brown, will you ship captain and take her to Sydney?" says he. "Let me choose my own mate and another white hand," says I, "for I don't hold with this Kanaka crew racket; give us all two months' advance to get our clothes and instruments out of pawn, and I'll take stock tonight, fill up stores, and get to sea tomorrow before dark!" That's what I said. "That's good enough," says the consul, "and you can count yourself damned lucky, Brown," says he. And he said it pretty meaningful-appearing, too. However, that's all one now. I'll ship Huish before the mast – of course I'll let him berth aft – and I'll ship you mate at seventy-five dollars and two months' advance.'

'Me mate? Why, I'm a landsman!' cried Herrick.

'Guess you've got to learn,' said the captain. 'You don't fancy I'm going to skip and leave you rotting on the beach perhaps? I'm not that sort, old man. And you're handy anyway; I've been shipmates with worse.'

'God knows I can't refuse,' said Herrick. 'God knows I thank you from my heart.'

'That's all right,' said the captain. 'But it ain't all.' He turned aside to light a cigar.

'What else is there?' asked the other, with a pang of undefinable alarm.

'I'm coming to that,' said Davis, and then paused a little. 'See here,' he began, holding out his cigar between his finger and thumb, 'suppose you figure up what this'll amount to. You don't catch on? Well, we get two months' advance; we can't get away from Papeete – our creditors wouldn't let us go – for less; it'll take us along about two months to get to Sydney; and when we get there, I just want to put it to you squarely: What the better are we?'

'We're off the beach at least,' said Herrick.

'I guess there's a beach at Sydney,' returned the captain; 'and I'll tell you one thing, Mr Herrick – I don't mean to try. No, *sir*! Sydney will never see me.'

'Speak out plain,' said Herrick.

'Plain Dutch,' replied the captain. 'I'm going to own that schooner. It's nothing new; it's done every year in the Pacific. Stephens stole a schooner the other day, didn't he? Hayes and Pease stole vessels all the time. And it's the making of the crowd of us. See here – you think of that cargo. Champagne! why, it's like as if it was put up on purpose. In Peru we'll sell that liquor off at the pier-head, and the schooner after it, if we can find a fool to buy her; and then light out for the mines. If you'll back me up, I stake my life I carry it through.'

'Captain,' said Herrick, with a quailing voice, 'don't do it!'

'I'm desperate,' returned Davis. 'I've got a chance; I may never get another. Herrick, say the word; back me up; I think we've starved together long enough for that.'

'I can't do it. I'm sorry. I can't do it. I've not fallen as low as that,' said Herrick, deadly pale.

'What did you say this morning?' said Davis. 'That you couldn't beg? It's the one thing or the other, my son.'

'Ah, but this is the jail!' cried Herrick. 'Don't tempt me. It's the jail.'

'Did you hear what the skipper said on board that schooner?'

pursued the captain. 'Well, I tell you he talked straight. The French have let us alone for a long time; it can't last longer; they've got their eye on us; and as sure as you live, in three weeks you'll be in jail whatever you do. I read it in the consul's face.'

'You forget, captain,' said the young man. 'There is another way. I can die; and to say truth, I think I should have died three years ago.'

The captain folded his arms and looked the other in the face. 'Yes,' said he, 'yes, you can cut your throat; that's a frozen fact; much good may it do you! And where do I come in?'

The light of a strange excitement came in Herrick's face. 'Both of us,' said he, 'both of us together. It's not possible you can enjoy this business. Come,' and he reached out a timid hand, 'a few strokes in the lagoon – and rest!'

'I tell you, Herrick, I'm 'most tempted to answer you the way the man does in the Bible, and say, "*Get thee behind me, Satan!*"' said the captain. 'What! you think I would go drown myself, and I got children starving? Enjoy it? No, by God, I do not enjoy it! but it's the row I've got to hoe, and I'll hoe it till I drop right here. I have three of them, you see, two boys and the one girl, Adar. The trouble is that you are not a parent yourself. I tell you, Herrick, I love you,' the man broke out; 'I didn't take to you at first, you were so anglified and tony, but I love you now; it's a man that loves you stands here and wrestles with you. I can't go to sea with the bummer alone; it's not possible. Go drown yourself, and there goes my last chance – the last chance of a poor miserable beast, earning a crust to feed his family. I can't do nothing but sail ships, and I've no papers. And here I get a chance, and you go back on me! Ah, you've no family, and that's where the trouble is!'

'I have indeed,' said Herrick.

'Yes, I know,' said the captain, 'you think so. But no man's got a family till he's got children. It's only the kids count. There's something about the little shavers ... I can't talk of them. And if you thought a cent about this father that I hear you talk of, or that sweetheart you were writing to this morning, you would feel like me. You would say, What matters laws, and God, and that? My folks are hard up, I belong to them, I'll get them bread, or, by God! I'll get them wealth, if I have to burn down London for it. That's what you would say. And I'll tell you more: your heart is saying so this living minute. I can see it in your face. You're thinking, Here's poor friendship for the man I've starved along of, and as for the girl that I set up to be in love with, here's a mighty limp kind of a love that won't carry me as far as 'most any man would go for a demijohn of whisky. There's not much *ro*mance to that love, anyway; it's not the kind they carry on about in songbooks. But what's the good of my carrying on talking, when it's all in your inside as plain as print? I put the question to you once for all. Are you going to desert me in my hour of need? – you know if I've deserted you – or will you give me your hand, and try a fresh deal, and go home (as like as not) a millionaire? Say no, and God pity me! Say yes, and I'll make the little ones pray for you every night on their bended knees. "God bless Mr Herrick!" that's what they'll say, one after the other, the old girl sitting there holding stakes at the foot of the bed, and the damned little innocents . . .' He broke off. 'I don't often rip out about the kids,' he said; 'but when I do, there's something fetches loose.'

'Captain,' said Herrick faintly, 'is there nothing else?'

'I'll prophesy if you like,' said the captain with renewed vigour. 'Refuse this, because you think yourself too honest, and before a month's out you'll be jailed for a sneak-thief. I give you the word fair. I can see it, Herrick, if you can't; you're breaking down. Don't think, if you refuse this chance, that you'll go on doing the evangelical; you're about through with your stock; and before you know where you are, you'll be right out on the other side. No, it's either this for you; or else it's Caledonia. I bet you never were there, and saw those white, shaved men, in their dust clothes and straw hats, prowling around in gangs in the lamplight at Noumea; they look like wolves, and they look like preachers, and they look like the sick; Huish is a daisy to the best of them. Well, there's your company. They're waiting for you, Herrick, and you got to go; and that's a prophecy.'

And as the man stood and shook through his great stature, he seemed indeed like one in whom the spirit of divination worked and might utter oracles. Herrick looked at him, and looked away; it seemed not decent to spy upon such agitation; and the young man's courage sank.

'You talk of going home,' he objected. 'We could never do that.'

'*We* could,' said the other. 'Captain Brown couldn't, nor Mr Hay, that shipped mate with him couldn't. But what's that to do with Captain Davis or Mr Herrick, you galoot?'

'But Hayes had these wild islands where he used to call,' came the next fainter objection.

'We have the wild islands of Peru,' retorted Davis. 'They were wild enough for Stephens, no longer agone than just last year. I guess they'll be wild enough for us.'

'And the crew?'

'All Kanakas. Come, I see you're right, old man. I see you'll stand by.' And the captain once more offered his hand.

'Have it your own way then,' said Herrick. 'I'll do it: a strange thing for my father's son. But I'll do it. I'll stand by you, man, for good or evil.'

'God bless you!' cried the captain, and stood silent. 'Herrick,' he added with a smile, 'I believe I'd have died in my tracks, if you'd said, No!'

And Herrick, looking at the man, half believed so also.

'And now we'll go break it to the bummer,' said Davis.

'I wonder how he'll take it,' said Herrick.

'Him? Jump at it!' was the reply.

Chapter 4

THE YELLOW FLAG

The schooner *Farallone* lay well out in the jaws of the pass, where the terrified pilot had made haste to bring her to her moorings and escape. Seen from the beach through the thin line of shipping, two objects stood conspicuous to seaward: the little isle, on the one hand, with its palms and the guns and batteries raised forty years before in defence of Queen Pomare's capital; the outcast *Farallone*, upon the other, banished to the threshold of the port, rolling there to her scuppers, and flaunting the plague-flag as she rolled. A few sea birds screamed and cried about the ship; and within easy range, a man-of-war guard boat hung off and on and glittered with the weapons of marines. The exuberant daylight and the blinding heaven of the tropics picked out and framed the pictures.

A neat boat, manned by natives in uniform, and steered by the doctor of the port, put from shore towards three of the afternoon, and pulled smartly for the schooner. The fore-sheets were heaped with sacks of flour, onions, and potatoes, perched among which was Huish dressed as a foremast hand; a heap of chests and cases impeded the action of the oarsmen; and in the stern, by the left hand of the doctor, sat Herrick, dressed in a fresh rig of slops, his brown beard trimmed to a point, a pile of paper novels on his lap, and nursing the while between his feet a chronometer, for which they had exchanged that of the *Farallone*, long since run down and the rate lost.

They passed the guard boat, exchanging hails with the boat-swain's mate in charge, and drew near at last to the forbidden ship. Not a cat stirred, there was no speech of man; and the sea being exceeding high outside, and the reef close to where the schooner lay, the clamour of the surf hung round her like the sound of battle.

'*Ohé la goëlette!*'* sang out the doctor, with his best voice.

Instantly, from the house where they had been stowing away stores, first Davis, and then the ragamuffin, swarthy crew made their appearance.

'Hullo, Hay, that you?' said the captain, leaning on the rail. 'Tell the old man to lay her alongside, as if she was eggs. There's a hell of a run of sea here, and his boat's brittle.'

The movement of the schooner was at that time more than usually violent. Now she heaved her side as high as a deep sea steamer's, and showed the flashing of her copper; now she swung swiftly toward the boat until her scuppers gurgled.

'I hope you have sea legs,' observed the doctor. 'You will require them.'

Indeed, to board the *Farallone*, in that exposed position where she lay, was an affair of some dexterity. The less precious goods were hoisted roughly in; the chronometer, after repeated failures, was passed gently and successfully from hand to hand; and there remained only the more difficult business of embarking Huish. Even that piece of dead weight (shipped A.B. at eighteen dollars, and described by the captain to the consul as an invaluable man) was at last hauled on board without mishap; and the doctor, with civil salutations, took his leave.

The three co-adventurers looked at each other, and Davis heaved a breath of relief.

'Now let's get this chronometer fixed,' said he, and led the way into the house. It was a fairly spacious place; two state-rooms and a good-sized pantry opened from the main cabin; the bulkheads were painted white, the floor laid with waxcloth. No litter, no sign of life remained; for the effects of the dead men had been disinfected and conveyed on shore. Only on the table, in a saucer, some sulphur burned, and the fumes set them coughing as they entered. The captain peered into the starboard stateroom, where the bed-clothes still lay tumbled in the bunk, the blanket flung back as they had flung it back from the disfigured corpse before its burial.

'Now, I told these niggers to tumble that truck overboard,' grumbled Davis. 'Guess they were afraid to lay hands on it.

Well, they've hosed the place out; that's as much as can be expected, I suppose. Huish, lay on to these blankets.'

'See you blooming well far enough first,' said Huish, drawing back.

'What's that?' snapped the captain. 'I'll tell you, my young friend, I think you make a mistake. I'm captain here.'

'Fat lot I care,' returned the clerk.

'That so?' said Davis. 'Then you'll berth forward with the niggers! Walk right out of this cabin.'

'Oh, I dessay!' said Huish. 'See any green in my eye? A lark's a lark.'

'Well, now, I'll explain this business, and you'll see (once for all) just precisely how much lark there is to it,' said Davis. 'I'm captain, and I'm going to be it. One thing of three. First, you take my orders here as cabin steward, in which case you mess with us. Or second, you refuse, and I pack you forward – and you get as quick as the word's said. Or, third and last, I'll signal that man-of-war and send you ashore under arrest for mutiny.'

'And, of course, I wouldn't blow the gaff? O no!' replied the jeering Huish.

'And who's to believe you, my son?' inquired the captain. 'No, *sir*! There ain't no lark about my captainising. Enough said. Up with these blankets.'

Huish was no fool, he knew when he was beaten; and he was no coward either, for he stepped to the bunk, took the infected bed-clothes fairly in his arms, and carried them out of the house without a check or tremor.

'I was waiting for the chance,' said Davis to Herrick. 'I needn't do the same with you, because you understand it for yourself.'

'Are you going to berth here?' asked Herrick, following the captain into the stateroom, where he began to adjust the chronometer in its place at the bed-head.

'Not much!' replied he. 'I guess I'll berth on deck. I don't know as I'm afraid, but I've no immediate use for confluent smallpox.'

'I don't know that I'm afraid either,' said Herrick. 'But the thought of these two men sticks in my throat; that captain and mate dying here, one opposite to the other. It's grim. I wonder what they said last?'

'Wiseman and Wishart?' said the captain. 'Probably mighty small potatoes. That's a thing a fellow figures out for himself one way, and the real business goes quite another. Perhaps Wiseman said, "Here old man, fetch up the gin, I'm feeling powerful rocky." And perhaps Wishart said, "Oh, hell!"'

'Well, that's grim enough,' said Herrick.

'And so it is,' said Davis. 'There; there's that chronometer fixed. And now it's about time to up anchor and clear out.'

He lit a cigar and stepped on deck.

'Here, you! What's *your* name?' he cried to one of the hands, a lean-flanked, clean-built fellow from some far western island, and of a darkness almost approaching to the African.

'Sally Day,' replied the man.

'Devil it is,' said the captain. 'Didn't know we had ladies on board. Well, Sally, oblige me by hauling down that rag there. I'll do the same for you another time.' He watched the yellow bunting as it was eased past the cross-trees and handed down on deck. 'You'll float no more on this ship,' he observed. 'Muster the people aft, Mr Hay,' he added, speaking unnecessarily loud, 'I've a word to say to them.'

It was with a singular sensation that Herrick prepared for the first time to address a crew. He thanked his stars indeed, that they were natives. But even natives, he reflected, might be critics too quick for such a novice as himself; they might perceive some lapse from that precise and cut-and-dry English which prevails on board a ship; it was even possible they understood no other; and he racked his brain, and overhauled his reminiscences of sea romance for some appropriate words.

'Here, men! tumble aft!' he said. 'Lively now! All hands aft!'

They crowded in the alleyway like sheep.

'Here they are, sir,' said Herrick.

For some time the captain continued to face the stern; then turned with ferocious suddenness on the crew, and seemed to enjoy their shrinking.

'Now,' he said, twisting his cigar in his mouth and toying with the spokes of the wheel, 'I'm Captain Brown. I command this ship. This is Mr Hay, first officer. The other white man is cabin steward, but he'll stand watch and do his trick. My orders shall be obeyed smartly. You savvy, "*smartly*"? There shall be no growling about the kaikai, which will be above allowance. You'll put a handle to the mate's name, and tack on "sir" to every order I give you. If you're smart and quick, I'll make this ship comfortable for all hands.' He took the cigar out of his mouth. 'If you're not,' he added, in a roaring voice, 'I'll make it a floating hell. Now, Mr Hay, we'll pick watches, if you please.'

'All right,' said Herrick.

'You will please use "sir" when you address me, Mr Hay,' said the captain. 'I'll take the lady. Step to starboard, Sally.' And then he whispered in Herrick's ear: 'take the old man.'

'I'll take you, there,' said Herrick.

'What's your name?' said the captain. 'What's that you say? Oh, that's no English; I'll have none of your highway gibberish on my ship. We'll call you old Uncle Ned, because you've got no wool on the top of your head, just the place where the wool ought to grow. Step to port, Uncle. Don't you hear Mr Hay has picked you? Then I'll take the white man. White Man, step to starboard. Now which of you two is the cook? You? Then Mr Hay takes your friend in the blue dungaree. Step to port, Dungaree. There, we know who we all are: Dungaree, Uncle Ned, Sally Day, White Man, and Cook. All F.F.V.'s I guess. And now, Mr Hay, we'll up anchor, if you please.'

'For Heaven's sake, tell me some of the words,' whispered Herrick.

An hour later, the *Farallone* was under all plain sail, the rudder hard a-port, and the cheerfully clanking windlass had brought the anchor home.

'All clear, sir,' cried Herrick from the bow.

The captain met her with the wheel, as she bounded like a stag from her repose, trembling and bending to the puffs. The guard boat gave a parting hail, the wake whitened and ran out; the *Farallone* was under weigh.

Her berth had been close to the pass. Even as she forged ahead Davis slewed her for the channel between the pier ends of the reef, the breakers sounding and whitening to either hand. Straight through the narrow band of blue, she shot to seaward: and the captain's heart exulted as he felt her tremble underfoot, and (looking back over the taffrail) beheld the roofs of Papeete changing position on the shore and the island mountains rearing higher in the wake.

But they were not yet done with the shore and the horror of the yellow flag. About midway of the pass, there was a cry and a scurry, a man was seen to leap upon the rail, and, throwing his arms over his head, to stoop and plunge into the sea.

'Steady as she goes,' the captain cried, relinquishing the wheel to Huish.

The next moment he was forward in the midst of the Kanakas, belaying pin in hand.

'Anybody else for shore?' he cried, and the savage trumpeting of his voice, no less than the ready weapon in his hand, struck fear in all. Stupidly they stared after their escaped companion, whose black head was visible upon the water, steering for the land. And the schooner meanwhile slipt like a racer through the pass, and met the long sea of the open ocean with a souse of spray.

'Fool that I was, not to have a pistol ready!' exclaimed Davis. 'Well, we go to sea short-handed, we can't help that. You have a lame watch of it, Mr Hay.'

'I don't see how we are to get along,' said Herrick.

'Got to,' said the captain. 'No more Tahiti for me.'

Both turned instinctively and looked astern. The fair island was unfolding mountain top on mountain top; Eimeo, on the port board, lifted her splintered pinnacles; and still the schooner raced to the open sea.

'Think!' cried the captain with a gesture, 'yesterday morning I danced for my breakfast like a poodle dog.'

Chapter 5

THE CARGO OF CHAMPAGNE

The ship's head was laid to clear Eimeo to the north, and the captain sat down in the cabin, with a chart, a ruler, and an epitome.

'East a half no'the,' said he, raising his face from his labours. 'Mr Hay, you'll have to watch your dead reckoning; I want every yard she makes on every hair's-breadth of a course. I'm going to knock a hole right straight through the Paumotus, and that's always a near touch. Now, if this South East Trade ever blew out of the S.E., which it don't, we might hope to lie within half a point of our course. Say we lie within a point of it. That'll just about weather Fakarava. Yes, sir, that's what we've got to do, if we tack for it. Brings us through this slush of little islands in the cleanest place: see?' And he showed where his ruler intersected the wide-lying labyrinth of the Dangerous Archipelago. 'I wish it was night, and I could put her about right now; we're losing time and easting. Well, we'll do our best. And if we don't fetch Peru, we'll bring up to Ecuador. All one, I guess. Depreciated dollars down, and no questions asked. A remarkable fine institootion, the South American don.'

Tahiti was already some way astern, the Diadem rising from among broken mountains – Eimeo was already close aboard, and stood black and strange against the golden splendour of the west – when the captain took his departure from the two islands, and the patent log was set.

Some twenty minutes later, Sally Day, who was continually leaving the wheel to peer in at the cabin clock, announced in a shrill cry 'Fo'bell,' and the cook was to be seen carrying the soup into the cabin.

'I guess I'll sit down and have a pick with you,' said Davis to

Herrick. 'By the time I've done, it'll be dark, and we'll clap the hooker on the wind for South America.'

In the cabin at one corner of the table, immediately below the lamp, and on the lee side of a bottle of champagne, sat Huish.

'What's this? Where did that come from?' asked the captain.

'It's fizz, and it came from the after-'old, if you want to know,' said Huish, and drained his mug.

'This'll never do,' exclaimed Davis, the merchant seaman's horror of breaking into cargo showing incongruously forth on board that stolen ship. 'There was never any good came of games like that.'

'You byby!' said Huish. 'A fellow would think (to 'ear him) we were on the square! And look 'ere, you've put this job up 'ansomely for me, 'aven't you? I'm to go on deck and steer while you two sit and guzzle, and I'm to go by nickname, and got to call you "sir" and "mister." Well, you look here, my bloke: I'll have fizz *ad lib.*, or it won't wash. I tell you that. And you know mighty well, you ain't got any man-of-war to signal now.'

Davis was staggered. 'I'd give fifty dollars this had never happened,' he said weakly.

'Well, it *'as* 'appened, you see,' returned Huish. 'Try some; it's devilish good.'

The Rubicon was crossed without another struggle. The captain filled a mug and drank.

'I wish it was beer,' he said with a sigh. 'But there's no denying it's the genuine stuff and cheap at the money. Now, Huish, you clear out and take your wheel.'

The little wretch had gained a point, and he was gay. 'Ay, ay, sir,' said he, and left the others to their meal.

'Pea soup!' exclaimed the captain. 'Blamed if I thought I should taste pea soup again!'

Herrick sat inert and silent. It was impossible after these months of hopeless want to smell the rough, high-spiced sea victuals without lust, and his mouth watered with desire of the champagne. It was no less impossible to have assisted at the scene between Huish and the captain, and not to perceive, with sudden bluntness, the gulf where he had fallen. He was a thief among thieves. He said it to himself. He could not touch the soup. If he had moved at all, it must have been to leave the table, throw himself overboard, and drown – an honest man.

'Here,' said the captain, 'you look sick, old man; have a drop of this.'

The champagne creamed and bubbled in the mug; its bright colour, its lively effervescence, seized his eye. 'It is too late to hesitate,' he thought; his hand took the mug instinctively; he drank, with unquenchable pleasure and desire of more; drained the vessel dry, and set it down with sparkling eyes.

'There is something in life after all!' he cried. 'I had forgot what it was like. Yes, even this is worth while. Wine, food, dry clothes – why, they're worth dying, worth hanging, for! Captain, tell me one thing: why aren't all the poor folk foot-pads?'

'Give it up,' said the captain.

'They must be damned good,' cried Herrick. 'There's something here beyond me. Think of that calaboose! Suppose we were sent suddenly back.' He shuddered as though stung by a convulsion, and buried his face in his clutching hands.

'Here, what's wrong with you?' cried the captain. There was no reply; only Herrick's shoulders heaved, so that the table was shaken. 'Take some more of this. Here, drink this. I order you to. Don't start crying when you're out of the wood.'

'I'm not crying,' said Herrick, raising his face and showing his dry eyes. 'It's worse than crying. It's the horror of that grave that we've escaped from.'

'Come now, you tackle your soup; that'll fix you,' said Davis kindly. 'I told you you were all broken up. You couldn't have stood out another week.'

'That's the dreadful part of it!' cried Herrick. 'Another week and I'd have murdered someone for a dollar! God! and I know that? And I'm still living? It's some beastly dream.'

'Quietly, quietly! Quietly does it, my son. Take your pea soup. Food, that's what you want,' said Davis.

The soup strengthened and quieted Herrick's nerves; another glass of wine, and a piece of pickled pork and fried banana completed what the soup began; and he was able once more to look the captain in the face.

'I didn't know I was so much run down,' he said.

'Well,' said Davis, 'you were as steady as a rock all day: now you've had a little lunch, you'll be as steady as a rock again.'

'Yes,' was the reply, 'I'm steady enough now, but I'm a queer kind of a first officer.'

'Shucks!' cried the captain. 'You've only got to mind the ship's course, and keep your slate to half a point. A babby could do that, let alone a college graduate like you. There ain't nothing *to* sailoring, when you come to look it in the face. And now we'll go and put her about. Bring the slate; we'll have to start our dead reckoning right away.'

The distance run since the departure was read off the log by the binnacle light and entered on the slate.

'Ready about,' said the captain. 'Give me the wheel, White Man, and you stand by the mainsheet. Boom tackle, Mr Hay, please, and then you can jump forward and attend head sails.'

'Ay, ay, sir,' responded Herrick.

'All clear forward?' asked Davis.

'All clear, sir.'

'Hard a-lee!' cried the captain. 'Haul in your slack as she comes,' he called to Huish. 'Haul in your slack, put your back into it; keep your feet out of the coils.' A sudden blow sent Huish flat along the deck, and the captain was in his place. 'Pick yourself up and keep the wheel hard over!' he roared. 'You wooden fool, you wanted to get killed, I guess. Draw the jib,' he cried a moment later; and then to Huish, 'Give me the wheel again, and see if you can coil that sheet.'

But Huish stood and looked at Davis with an evil countenance. 'Do you know you struck me?' said he.

'Do you know I saved your life?' returned the other, not deigning to look at him, his eyes travelling instead between the compass and the sails. 'Where would you have been, if that boom had swung out and you bundled in the clack? No, *sir*, we'll have no more of you at the mainsheet. Seaport towns are full of mainsheet-men; they hop upon one leg, my son, what's left of them, and the rest are dead. (Set your boom tackle, Mr Hay.) Struck you, did I? Lucky for you I did.'

'Well,' said Huish slowly, 'I daresay there may be somethink in that. 'Ope there is.' He turned his back elaborately on the captain, and entered the house, where the speedy explosion of a champagne cork showed he was attending to his comfort.

Herrick came aft to the captain. 'How is she doing now?' he asked.

'East and by no'the a half no'the,' said Davis. 'It's about as good as I expected.'

'What'll the hands think of it?' said Herrick.

'Oh, they don't think. They ain't paid to,' says the captain.

'There was something wrong, was there not? between you and—' Herrick paused.

'That's a nasty little beast, that's a biter,' replied the captain, shaking his head. 'But so long as you and me hang in, it don't matter.'

Herrick lay down in the weather alleyway; the night was cloudless, the movement of the ship cradled him, he was oppressed besides by the first generous meal after so long a time of famine; and he was recalled from deep sleep by the voice of Davis singing out: 'Eight bells!'

He rose stupidly, and staggered aft, where the captain gave him the wheel.

'By the wind,' said the captain. 'It comes a little puffy; when you get a heavy puff, steal all you can to windward, but keep her a good full.'

He stepped towards the house, paused and hailed the forecastle.

'Got such a thing as a concertina forward?' said he. 'Bully for you, Uncle Ned. Fetch it aft, will you?'

The schooner steered very easy; and Herrick, watching the moon-whitened sails, was overpowered by drowsiness. A sharp report from the cabin startled him; a third bottle had been opened; and Herrick remembered the *Sea Ranger* and Fourteen Island Group. Presently the notes of the accordion sounded, and then the captain's voice:

> 'O honey, with our pockets full of money,
> We will trip, trip, trip, we will trip it on the quay,
> And I will dance with Kate, and Tom will dance with Sall,
> When we're all back from South Amerikee.'

So it went to its quaint air; and the watch below lingered and listened by the forward door, and Uncle Ned was to be seen in the moonlight nodding time; and Herrick smiled at the wheel, his anxieties a while forgotten. Song followed song; another cork exploded; there were voices raised, as though the pair in the cabin were in disagreement; and presently it seemed the breach was healed; for it was now the voice of Huish that struck up, to the captain's accompaniment—

> 'Up in a balloon, boys,
> Up in a balloon,
> All among the little stars
> And round about the moon.'

A wave of nausea overcame Herrick at the wheel. He wondered why the air, the words (which were yet written with a certain knack), and the voice and accent of the singer, should all jar his spirit like a file on a man's teeth. He sickened at the thought of his two comrades drinking away their reason upon stolen wine, quarrelling and hiccupping and waking up, while the doors of the prison yawned for them in the near future. 'Shall I have sold my honour for nothing?' he thought; and a heat of rage and resolution glowed in his bosom – rage against his comrades – resolution to carry through this business if it might be carried; pluck profit out of shame, since the shame at least was now inevitable; and come home, home from South America – how did the song go? – 'with his pockets full of money':

> 'O honey, with our pockets full of money,
> We will trip, trip, trip, we will trip it on the quay:'

so the words ran in his head; and the honey took on visible form, the quay rose before him and he knew it for the lamplit Embankment, and he saw the lights of Battersea bridge bestride the sullen river. All through the remainder of his trick, he stood entranced, reviewing the past. He had been always true to his love, but not always sedulous to recall her. In the growing calamity of his life, she had swum more distant, like the moon in mist. The letter of farewell, the dishonourable hope that had surprised and corrupted him in his distress, the changed scene, the sea, the night and the music – all stirred him to the roots of manhood. 'I *will* win her,' he thought, and ground his teeth. 'Fair or foul, what matters if I win her?'

'Fo' bell, matey. I think um fo' bell' – he was suddenly recalled by these words in the voice of Uncle Ned.

'Look in at the clock, Uncle,' said he. He would not look himself, from horror of the tipplers.

'Him past, matey,' repeated the Hawaiian.

'So much the better for you, Uncle,' he replied; and he gave up the wheel, repeating the directions as he had received them.

He took two steps forward and remembered his dead reckoning. 'How has she been heading?' he thought; and he flushed from head to foot. He had not observed or had forgotten; here was the old incompetence; the slate must be filled up by guess. 'Never again!' he vowed to himself in silent fury, 'never again. It shall be no fault of mine if this miscarry.' And for the remainder of his watch, he stood close by Uncle Ned, and read the face of the compass as perhaps he had never read a letter from his sweetheart.

All the time, and spurring him to the more attention, song, loud talk, fleering laughter and the occasional popping of a cork, reached his ears from the interior of the house; and when the port watch was relieved at midnight, Huish and the captain appeared upon the quarter-deck with flushed faces and uneven steps, the former laden with bottles, the latter with two tin mugs. Herrick silently passed them by. They hailed him in thick voices, he made no answer, they cursed him for a churl, he paid no heed although his belly quivered with disgust and rage. He closed-to the door of the house behind him, and cast himself on a locker in the cabin – not to sleep he thought – rather to think and to despair. Yet he had scarce turned twice on his uneasy bed, before a drunken voice hailed him in the ear, and he must go on deck again to stand the morning watch.

The first evening set the model for those that were to follow. Two cases of champagne scarce lasted the four-and-twenty hours, and almost the whole was drunk by Huish and the captain. Huish seemed to thrive on the excess; he was never sober, yet never wholly tipsy; the food and the sea air had soon healed him of his disease, and he began to lay on flesh. But with Davis things went worse. In the drooping, unbuttoned figure that sprawled all day upon the lockers, tippling and reading novels; in the fool who made of the evening watch a public carouse on the quarter-deck, it would have been hard to recognise the vigorous seaman of Papeete roads. He kept himself reasonably well in hand till he had taken the sun and yawned and blotted through his calculations; but from the moment he rolled up the chart, his hours were passed in slavish self-indulgence or in hoggish slumber. Every other branch of his duty was neglected, except maintaining a stern discipline about the dinner table. Again and again Herrick would hear the cook called aft, and see him running with fresh tins, or carrying away again a meal that had been totally condemned. And the more the captain became sunk in drunkenness, the more delicate his palate showed itself. Once, in the forenoon, he had a bo'sun's chair rigged over the rail, stripped to his trousers, and went overboard with a pot of paint. 'I don't like the way this schooner's painted,' said he, 'and I've taken a down upon her name.' But he tired of it in half an hour, and the schooner went on her way with an incongruous patch of colour on the stern, and the word *Farallone* part obliterated and part looking through. He refused to stand either the middle or the morning watch. It was fine-weather sailing, he said; and asked, with a laugh, 'Who ever heard of the old man standing watch himself?' To the dead reckoning which Herrick still tried to keep, he would pay not the least attention nor afford the least assistance.

'What do we want of dead reckoning?' he asked. 'We get the sun all right, don't we?'

'We mayn't get it always though,' objected Herrick. 'And you told me yourself you weren't sure of the chronometer.'

'Oh, there ain't no flies in the chronometer!' cried Davis.

'Oblige me so far, captain,' said Herrick stiffly. 'I am anxious to keep this reckoning, which is a part of my duty; I do not know what to allow for current, nor how to allow for it. I am too inexperienced; and I beg of you to help me.'

'Never discourage zealous officer,' said the captain, unrolling the chart again, for Herrick had taken him over his day's work and while he was still partly sober. 'Here it is: look for yourself; anything from west to west no'the-west, and anyways from five to twenty-five miles. That's what the A'm'ralty chart says; I guess you don't expect to get on ahead of your own Britishers?'

'I am trying to do my duty, Captain Brown,' said Herrick, with a dark flush, 'and I have the honour to inform you that I don't enjoy being trifled with.'

'What in thunder do you want?' roared Davis. 'Go and look at the blamed wake. If you're trying to do your duty, why don't you go and do it? I guess it's no business of mine to go and stick my head over the ship's rump? I guess it's yours. And I'll tell you what it is, my fine fellow, I'll trouble you not to come the dude over me. You're insolent, that's what's wrong with you. Don't you crowd me, Mr Herrick, Esquire.'

Herrick tore up his papers, threw them on the floor, and left the cabin.

'He's turned a bloomin' swot, ain't he?' sneered Huish.

'He thinks himself too good for his company, that's what ails Herrick, Esquire,' raged the captain. 'He thinks I don't understand when he comes the heavy swell. Won't sit down with us, won't he? won't say a civil word? I'll serve the son of a gun as he deserves. By God, Huish, I'll show him whether he's too good for John Davis!'

'Easy with the names, cap',' said Huish, who was always the more sober. 'Easy over the stones, my boy!'

'All right, I will. You're a good sort, Huish. I didn't take to you at first, but I guess you're right enough. Let's open another bottle,' said the captain; and that day, perhaps because he was excited by the quarrel, he drank more recklessly, and by four o'clock was stretched insensible upon the locker.

Herrick and Huish supped alone, one after the other, opposite his flushed and snorting body. And if the sight killed Herrick's hunger, the isolation weighed so heavily on the clerk's spirit, that he was scarce risen from table ere he was currying favour with his former comrade.

Herrick was at the wheel when he approached, and Huish leaned confidentially across the binnacle.

'I say, old chappie,' he said, 'you and me don't seem to be such pals somehow.'

Herrick gave her a spoke or two in silence; his eye, as it skirted from the needle to the luff of the foresail, passed the man by without speculation. But Huish was really dull, a thing he could support with difficulty, having no resources of his own. The idea of a private talk with Herrick, at this stage of their relations, held out particular inducements to a person of his character. Drink besides, as it renders some men hyper-sensitive, made Huish callous. And it would almost have required a blow to make him quit his purpose.

'Pretty business, ain't it?' he continued; 'Dyvis on the lush? Must say I thought you gave it 'im A1 today. He didn't like it a bit; took on hawful after you were gone.— "'Ere," says I, "'old on, easy on the lush," I says. "'Errick was right, and you know it. Give 'im a chanst," I says.— "'Uish," sezee, "don't you gimme no more of your jaw, or I'll knock your bloomin' eyes out." Well, wot can I do, 'Errick? But I tell you, I don't 'arf like it. It looks to me like the *Sea Rynger* over again.'

Still Herrick was silent.

'Do you 'ear me speak?' asked Huish sharply. 'You're pleasant, ain't you?'

'Stand away from that binnacle,' said Herrick.

The clerk looked at him, long and straight and black; his figure seemed to writhe like that of a snake about to strike; then he turned on his heel, went back to the cabin and opened a bottle of champagne. When eight bells were cried, he slept on the floor beside the captain on the locker; and of the whole starboard watch, only Sally Day appeared upon the summons. The mate proposed to stand the watch with him, and let Uncle Ned lie down; it would make twelve hours on deck, and probably sixteen, but in this fair-weather sailing, he might safely sleep between his tricks of wheel, leaving orders to be called on any sign of squalls. So far he could trust the men, between whom and himself a close relation had sprung up. With Uncle Ned he held long nocturnal conversations, and the old man told him his simple and hard story of exile, suffering, and injustice among cruel whites. The cook, when he found Herrick messed alone, produced for him unexpected and sometimes unpalatable dainties, of which he forced himself to eat. And one day, when he was forward, he was surprised to feel a caressing hand run down his shoulder, and to hear the voice of Sally Day crooning in his ear: 'You gootch man!' He turned, and, choking down a sob, shook hands with the negrito. They were kindly, cheery, childish souls. Upon the Sunday each brought forth his separate Bible – for they were all men of alien speech even to each other, and Sally Day communicated with his mates in English only, each read or made believe to read his chapter, Uncle Ned with spectacles on his nose; and they would all join together in the singing of missionary hymns. It was thus a cutting reproof to compare the islanders and the whites aboard the *Farallone*. Shame ran in Herrick's blood to remember what employment he was on, and to see these poor souls – and even Sally Day, the child of cannibals, in all likelihood a cannibal himself – so faithful to what they knew of good. The fact that he was held in grateful favour by these innocents served like blinders to his conscience, and there were times when he was inclined, with Sally Day, to call himself a good man. But the height of his favour was only now to appear. With one voice, the crew protested; ere Herrick knew what they were doing, the cook was aroused and came a willing volunteer; all hands clustered about their mate with expostulations and caresses; and he was bidden to lie down and take his customary rest without alarm.

'He tell you tlue,' said Uncle Ned. 'You sleep. Evely man hae he do all light. Evely man he like you too much.'

Herrick struggled, and gave way; choked upon some trivial words of gratitude; and walked to the side of the house, against which he leaned, struggling with emotion.

Uncle Ned presently followed him and begged him to lie down.

'It's no use, Uncle Ned,' he replied. 'I couldn't sleep. I'm knocked over with all your goodness.'

'Ah, no call me Uncle Ned no mo'!' cried the old man. 'No my name! My name Taveeta, all-e-same Taveeta King of Islael. Wat for he call that Hawaii? I think no savvy nothing – all-e-same Wise-a-mana.'

It was the first time the name of the late captain had been mentioned, and Herrick grasped the occasion. The reader shall be spared Uncle Ned's unwieldy dialect, and learn in less embarrassing English, the sum of what he now communicated. The ship had scarce cleared the Golden Gates before the captain and mate had entered on a career of drunkenness, which was scarcely interrupted by their malady and only closed by death. For days and weeks they had encountered neither land nor ship; and seeing themselves lost on the huge deep with their insane conductors, the natives had drunk deep of terror.

At length they made a low island, and went in; and Wiseman and Wishart landed in the boat.

There was a great village, a very fine village, and plenty Kanakas in that place; but all mighty serious; and from every here and there in the back parts of the settlement, Taveeta heard the sounds of island lamentation. 'I no savvy *talk* that island,' said he. 'I savvy hear um *cly*. I think, Hum! too many people die here!' But upon Wiseman and Wishart the significance of that barbaric keening was lost. Full of bread and drink, they rollicked along unconcerned, embraced the girls who had scarce energy to repel them, took up and joined (with drunken voices) in the death wail, and at last (on what they took to be an invitation) entered under the roof of a house in which was a considerable concourse of people sitting silent. They stooped below the eaves, flushed and laughing; within a minute they came forth again with changed faces and silent tongues; and as the press severed to make way for them, Taveeta was able to perceive, in the deep shadow of the house, the sick man raising from his mat a head already defeatured by disease. The two tragic triflers fled without hesitation for their boat, screaming on Taveeta to make haste; they came aboard with all speed of oars, raised anchor and crowded sail upon the ship with blows and curses, and were at sea again — and again drunk — before sunset. A week after, and the last of the two had been committed to the deep. Herrick asked Taveeta where that island was, and he replied that, by what he gathered of folks' talk as they went up together from the beach, he supposed it must be one of the Paumotus. This was in itself probable enough, for the Dangerous Archipelago had been swept that year from east to west by devastating smallpox; but Herrick thought it a strange course to lie from Sydney. Then he remembered the drink.

'Were they not surprised when they made the island?' he asked.

'Wise-a-mana he say "dam! what this?"' was the reply.

'O, that's it then,' said Herrick. 'I don't believe they knew where they were.'

'I think so too,' said Uncle Ned. 'I think no savvy. This one mo' betta,' he added, pointing to the house where the drunken captain slumbered: 'Take-a-sun all-e-time.'

The implied last touch completed Herrick's picture of the life and death of his two predecessors; of their prolonged, sordid, sodden sensuality as they sailed, they knew not whither, on their last cruise. He held but a twinkling and unsure belief in any future state; the thought of one of punishment he derided; yet for him (as for all) there dwelt a horror about the end of the brutish man. Sickness fell upon him at the image thus called up; and when he compared it with the scene in which himself was acting, and considered the doom that seemed to brood upon the schooner, a horror that was almost superstitious fell upon him. And yet the strange thing was, he did not falter. He who had proved his incapacity in so many fields, being now falsely placed amid duties which he did not understand, without help, and it might be said without countenance, had hitherto surpassed expectation; and even the shameful misconduct and shocking disclosures of that night seemed but to nerve and strengthen him. He had sold his honour; he vowed it should not be in vain; 'it shall be no fault of mine if this miscarry,' he repeated. And in his heart he wondered at himself. Living rage no doubt supported him; no doubt also, the sense of the last cast, of the ships burned, of all doors closed but one, which is so strong a tonic to the merely weak, and so deadly a depressant to the merely cowardly.

For some time the voyage went otherwise well. They weathered Fakarava with one board; and the wind holding well to the southward and blowing fresh, they passed between Ranaka and Ratiu, and ran some days north-east by east-half-east under the lee of Takume and Honden,* neither of which they made. In about 14° South and between 134° and 135° West, it fell a dead calm with rather a heavy sea. The captain refused to take in sail, the helm was lashed, no watch was set, and the *Farallone* rolled and banged for three days, according to observation, in almost the same place. The fourth morning, a little before day, a breeze sprang up and rapidly freshened. The captain had drunk hard the night before; he was far from sober when he was roused; and when he came on deck for the first time at half-past eight, it was plain he had already drunk deep again at breakfast. Herrick avoided his eye; and resigned the deck with indignation to a man more than half-seas over.

By the loud commands of the captain and the singing out of fellows at the ropes, he could judge from the house that sail was being crowded on the ship; relinquished his half-eaten breakfast; and came on deck again, to find the main and the jib topsails set, and both watches and the cook turned out to hand the staysail. The *Farallone* lay already far over; the sky was obscured with misty scud; and from the windward an ominous squall came flying up, broadening and blackening as it rose.

Fear thrilled in Herrick's vitals. He saw death hard by; and if not death, sure ruin. For if the *Farallone* lived through the coming squall, she must surely be dismasted. With that their enterprise was at an end, and they themselves bound prisoners

to the very evidence of their crime. The greatness of the peril
and his own alarm sufficed to silence him. Pride, wrath, and
shame raged without issue in his mind; and he shut his teeth
and folded his arms close.

The captain sat in the boat to windward, bellowing orders
and insults, his eyes glazed, his face deeply congested; a bottle
set between his knees, a glass in his hand half empty. His back
was to the squall, and he was at first intent upon the setting of
the sail. When that was done, and the great trapezium of canvas
had begun to draw and to trail the lee-rail of the *Farallone* level
with the foam, he laughed out an empty laugh, drained his glass,
sprawled back among the lumber in the boat, and fetched out a
crumpled novel.

Herrick watched him, and his indignation glowed red hot. He
glanced to windward where the squall already whitened the near
sea and heralded its coming with a singular and dismal sound.
He glanced at the steersman, and saw him clinging to the spokes
with a face of a sickly blue. He saw the crew were running to
their stations without orders. And it seemed as if something
broke in his brain; and the passion of anger, so long restrained,
so long eaten in secret, burst suddenly loose and shook him like
a sail. He stepped across to the captain and smote his hand
heavily on the drunkard's shoulder.

'You brute,' he said, in a voice that tottered, 'look behind
you!'

'Wha's that?' cried Davis, bounding in the boat and upsetting
the champagne.

'You lost the *Sea Ranger* because you were a drunken sot,'
said Herrick. 'Now you're going to lose the *Farallone*. You're
going to drown here the same way as you drowned others, and
be damned. And your daughter shall walk the streets, and your
sons be thieves like their father.'

For the moment, the words struck the captain white and
foolish. 'My God!' he cried, looking at Herrick as upon a ghost;
'my God, Herrick!'

'Look behind you, then!' reiterated the assailant.

The wretched man, already partly sobered, did as he was told, and in the same breath of time leaped to his feet. 'Down staysail!' he trumpeted. The hands were thrilling for the order, and the great sail came with a run, and fell half overboard among the racing foam. 'Jib topsail-halyards! Let the stays'l be,' he said again.

But before it was well uttered, the squall shouted aloud and fell, in a solid mass of wind and rain commingled, on the *Farallone*; and she stooped under the blow, and lay like a thing dead. From the mind of Herrick reason fled; he clung in the weather rigging, exulting; he was done with life, and he gloried in the release; he gloried in the wild noises of the wind and the choking onslaught of the rain; he gloried to die so, and now, amid this coil of the elements. And meanwhile, in the waist up to his knees in water – so low the schooner lay – the captain was hacking at the foresheet with a pocket knife. It was a question of seconds, for the *Farallone* drank deep of the encroaching seas. But the hand of the captain had the advance; the foresail boom tore apart the last strands of the sheet and crashed to leeward; the *Farallone* leaped up into the wind and righted; and the peak and throat halyards, which had long been let go, began to run at the same instant.

For some ten minutes more she careered under the impulse of the squall; but the captain was now master of himself and of his ship, and all danger at an end. And then, sudden as a trick change upon the stage, the squall blew by, the wind dropped into light airs, the sun beamed forth again upon the tattered schooner; and the captain, having secured the foresail boom and set a couple of hands to the pump, walked aft, sober, a little pale, and with the sodden end of a cigar still stuck between his teeth even as the squall had found it. Herrick followed him; he could scarce recall the violence of his late emotions, but he felt there was a scene to go through, and he was anxious and even eager to go through with it.

The captain, turning at the house end, met him face to face, and averted his eyes. 'We've lost the two tops'ls and the stays'l,' he gabbled. 'Good business, we didn't lose any sticks. I guess you think we're all the better without the kites.'

'That's not what I'm thinking,' said Herrick, in a voice strangely quiet, that yet echoed confusion in the captain's mind.

'I know that,' he cried, holding up his hand. 'I know what you're thinking. No use to say it now. I'm sober.'

'I have to say it, though,' returned Herrick.

'Hold on, Herrick; you've said enough,' said Davis. 'You've said what I would take from no man breathing but yourself; only I know it's true.'

'I have to tell you, Captain Brown,' pursued Herrick, 'that I resign my position as mate. You can put me in irons or shoot me, as you please; I will make no resistance – only, I decline in any way to help or to obey you; and I suggest you should put Mr Huish in my place. He will make a worthy first officer to your captain, sir.' He smiled, bowed, and turned to walk forward.

'Where are you going, Herrick?' cried the captain, detaining him by the shoulder.

'To berth forward with the men, sir,' replied Herrick, with the same hateful smile. 'I've been long enough aft here with you – gentlemen.'

'You're wrong there,' said Davis. 'Don't you be too quick with me; there ain't nothing wrong but the drink – it's the old story, man! Let me get sober once, and then you'll see,' he pleaded.

'Excuse me, I desire to see no more of you,' said Herrick.

The captain groaned aloud. 'You know what you said about my children?' he broke out.

'By rote. In case you wish me to say it you again?' asked Herrick.

'Don't!' cried the captain, clapping his hands to his ears. 'Don't make me kill a man I care for! Herrick, if you see me put a glass to my lips again till we're ashore, I give you leave to put a bullet through me; I beg you to do it! You're the only man aboard whose carcase is worth losing; do you think I don't know that? do you think I ever went back on you? I always knew you were in the right of it – drunk or sober, I knew that.

What do you want? – an oath? Man, you're clever enough to see that this is sure-enough earnest.'

'Do you mean there shall be no more drinking?' asked Herrick, 'neither by you nor Huish? that you won't go on stealing my profits and drinking my champagne that I gave my honour for? and that you'll attend to your duties, and stand watch and watch, and bear your proper share of the ship's work, instead of leaving it all on the shoulders of a landsman, and making yourself the butt and scoff of native seamen? Is that what you mean? If it is, be so good as to say it categorically.'

'You put these things in a way hard for a gentleman to swallow,' said the captain. 'You wouldn't have me say I was ashamed of myself? Trust me this once; I'll do the square thing, and there's my hand on it.'

'Well, I'll try it once,' said Herrick. 'Fail me again . . .'

'No more now!' interrupted Davis. 'No more, old man! Enough said. You've a riling tongue when your back's up, Herrick. Just be glad we're friends again, the same as what I am; and go tender on the raws; I'll see as you don't repent it. We've been mighty near death this day – don't say whose fault it was! – pretty near hell, too, I guess. We're in a mighty bad line of life, us two, and ought to go easy with each other.'

He was maundering; yet it seemed as if he were maundering with some design, beating about the bush of some communication that he feared to make, or perhaps only talking against time in terror of what Herrick might say next. But Herrick had now spat his venom; his was a kindly nature, and, content with his triumph, he had now begun to pity. With a few soothing words, he sought to conclude the interview, and proposed that they should change their clothes.

'Not right yet,' said Davis. 'There's another thing I want to tell you first. You know what you said about my children? I want to tell you why it hit me so hard; I kind of think you'll feel bad about it too. It's about my little Adar. You hadn't ought to have quite said that – but of course I know you didn't know. She – she's dead, you see.'

'Why, Davis!' cried Herrick. 'You've told me a dozen times she was alive! Clear your head, man! This must be the drink.'

"No, *sir*,' said Davis. 'She's dead. Died of a bowel complaint. That was when I was away in the brig *Oregon*. She lies in Portland, Maine. "Adar, only daughter of Captain John Davis and Mariar his wife, aged five." I had a doll for her on board. I never took the paper off'n that doll, Herrick; it went down the way it was with the *Sea Ranger*, that day I was damned.'

The Captain's eyes were fixed on the horizon, he talked with an extraordinary softness but a complete composure; and Herrick looked upon him with something that was almost terror.

'Don't think I'm crazy neither,' resumed Davis. 'I've all the cold sense that I know what to do with. But I guess a man that's unhappy's like a child; and this is a kind of a child's game of mine. I never could act up to the plain-cut truth, you see; so I pretend. And I warn you square; as soon as we're through with this talk, I'll start in again with the pretending. Only, you see, she can't walk no streets,' added the captain, 'couldn't even make out to live and get that doll!'

Herrick laid a tremulous hand upon the captain's shoulder.

'Don't do that!' cried Davis, recoiling from the touch. 'Can't you see I'm all broken up the way it is? Come along, then; come along, old man; you can put your trust in me right through; come along and get dry clothes.'

They entered the cabin, and there was Huish on his knees prising open a case of champagne.

''Vast, there!' cried the captain. 'No more of that. No more drinking on this ship.'

'Turned teetotal, 'ave you?' inquired Huish. 'I'm agreeable. About time, eh? Bloomin' nearly lost another ship, I fancy.' He took out a bottle and began calmly to burst the wire with the spike of a corkscrew.

'Do you hear me speak?' cried Davis.

'I suppose I do. You speak loud enough,' said Huish. 'The trouble is that I don't care.'

Herrick plucked the captain's sleeve. 'Let him free now,' he said. 'We've had all we want this morning.'

'Let him have it then,' said the captain. 'It's his last.'

By this time the wire was open, the string was cut, the head of gilded paper was torn away; and Huish waited, mug in hand, expecting the usual explosion. It did not follow. He eased the cork with his thumb; still there was no result. At last he took the screw and drew it. It came out very easy and with scarce a sound.

''Illo!' said Huish. ''Ere's a bad bottle.'

He poured some of the wine into the mug; it was colourless and still. He smelt and tasted it.

'W'y, wot's this?' he said. 'It's water!'

If the voice of trumpets had suddenly sounded about the ship in the midst of the sea, the three men in the house could scarcely have been more stunned than by this incident. The mug passed round; each sipped, each smelt of it; each stared at the bottle in its glory of gold paper as Crusoe may have stared at the footprint; and their minds were swift to fix upon a common apprehension. The difference between a bottle of champagne and a bottle of water is not great; between a shipload of one or the other lay the whole scale from riches to ruin.

A second bottle was broached. There were two cases standing ready in a stateroom; these two were brought out, broken open, and tested. Still with the same result: the contents were still colourless and tasteless, and dead as the rain in a beached fishing-boat.

'Crikey!' said Huish.

'Here, let's sample the hold!' said the captain, mopping his brow with a back-handed sweep; and the three stalked out of the house, grim and heavy-footed.

All hands were turned out; two Kanakas were sent below, another stationed at a purchase; and Davis, axe in hand, took his place beside the coamings.

'Are you going to let the men know?' whispered Herrick.

'Damn the men!' said Davis. 'It's beyond that. We've got to know ourselves.'

Three cases were sent on deck and sampled in turn; from each bottle, as the captain smashed it with the axe, the champagne ran bubbling and creaming.

'Go deeper, can't you?' cried Davis to the Kanakas in the hold.

The command gave the signal for a disastrous change. Case after case came up, bottle after bottle was burst and bled mere water. Deeper yet, and they came upon a layer where there was scarcely so much as the intention to deceive; where the cases were no longer branded, the bottles no longer wired or papered, where the fraud was manifest and stared them in the face.

'Here's about enough of this foolery!' said Davis. 'Stow back the cases in the hold, Uncle, and get the broken crockery overboard. Come with me,' he added to his co-adventurers, and led the way back into the cabin.

Chapter 6
THE PARTNERS

Each took a side of the fixed table; it was the first time they had sat down at it together; but now all sense of incongruity, all memory of differences, was quite swept away by the presence of the common ruin.

'Gentlemen,' said the captain, after a pause, and with very much the air of a chairman opening a board-meeting, 'we're sold.'

Huish broke out in laughter. 'Well, if this ain't the 'ighest old rig!' he cried. 'And Dyvis, 'ere, who thought he had got up so bloomin' early in the mornin'! We've stolen a cargo of spring water! Oh, my crikey!' and he squirmed with mirth.

The captain managed to screw out a phantom smile.

'Here's Old Man Destiny again,' said he to Herrick, 'but this time I guess he's kicked the door right in.'

Herrick only shook his head.

'O Lord, it's rich!' laughed Huish. 'It would really be a scrumptious lark if it 'ad 'appened to somebody else! And wot are we to do next? Oh, my eye! with this bloomin' schooner, too?'

'That's the trouble,' said Davis. 'There's only one thing certain: it's no use carting this old glass and ballast to Peru. No, *sir*, we're in a hole.'

'O my, and the merchant!' cried Huish; 'the man that made this shipment! He'll get the news by the mail brigantine; and he'll think of course we're making straight for Sydney.'

'Yes, he'll be a sick merchant,' said the captain. 'One thing: this explains the Kanaka crew. If you're going to lose a ship, I would ask no better myself than a Kanaka crew. But there's one thing it don't explain; it don't explain why she came down Tahiti ways.'

'W'y, to lose her, you byby!' said Huish.

'A lot you know,' said the captain. 'Nobody wants to lose a schooner; they want to lose her *on her course*, you skeericks! You seem to think underwriters haven't got enough sense to come in out of the rain.'

'Well,' said Herrick, 'I can tell you (I am afraid) why she came so far to the eastward. I had it of Uncle Ned. It seems these two unhappy devils, Wiseman and Wishart, were drunk on the champagne from the beginning – and died drunk at the end.'

The captain looked on the table.

'They lay in their two bunks, or sat here in this damned house,' he pursued, with rising agitation, 'filling their skins with the accursed stuff, till sickness took them. As they sickened and the fever rose, they drank the more. They lay here howling and groaning, drunk and dying, all in one. They didn't know where they were, they didn't care. They didn't even take the sun, it seems.'

'Not take the sun?' cried the captain, looking up. 'Sacred Billy! what a crowd!'

'Well, it don't matter to Joe!' said Huish. 'Wot are Wiseman and the t'other buffer to us?'

'A good deal, too,' says the captain. 'We're their heirs, I guess.'

'It is a great inheritance,' said Herrick.

'Well, I don't know about that,' returned Davis. 'Appears to me as if it might be worse. 'Tain't worth what the cargo would have been of course, at least not money down. But I'll tell you what it appears to figure up to. Appears to me as if it amounted to about the bottom dollar of the man in 'Frisco.'

''Old on,' said Huish. 'Give a fellow time; 'ow's this, umpire?'

'Well, my sons,' pursued the captain, who seemed to have recovered his assurance, 'Wiseman and Wishart were to be paid for casting away this old schooner and its cargo. We're going to cast away the schooner right enough; and I'll make it my private business to see that we get paid. What were W. and W. to get? That's more'n I can tell. But W. and W. went into this business themselves, they were on the crook. Now *we're* on the square, *we* only stumbled into it; and that merchant has just got to squeal, and I'm the man to see that he squeals good. No, *sir*! there's some stuffing to this *Farallone* racket after all.'

'Go it, cap!' cried Huish. 'Yoicks! Forrard! 'Old 'ard! There's your style for the money! Blow me if I don't prefer this to the hother.'

'I do not understand,' said Herrick. 'I have to ask you to excuse me; I do not understand.'

'Well now, see here, Herrick,' said Davis, 'I'm going to have a word with you anyway upon a different matter, and it's good that Huish should hear it too. We're done with this boozing business, and we ask your pardon for it right here and now. We have to thank you for all you did for us while we were making hogs of ourselves; you'll find me turn-to all right in future; and as for the wine, which I grant we stole from you, I'll take stock and see you paid for it. That's good enough, I believe. But what I want to point out to you is this. The old game was a risky game. The new game's as safe as running a Vienna Bakery. We just put this *Farallone* before the wind, and run till we're well to looard of our port of departure and reasonably well up with some other place, where they have an American Consul. Down goes the *Farallone*, and good-bye to her! A day or so in the boat; the consul packs us home, at Uncle Sam's expense, to 'Frisco; and if that merchant don't put the dollars down, you come to me!'

'But I thought,' began Herrick; and then broke out; 'oh, let's get on to Peru!'

'Well, if you're going to Peru for your health, I won't say no!' replied the captain. 'But for what other blame' shadow of a reason you should want to go there, gets me clear. We don't want to go there with this cargo; I don't know as old bottles is a lively article anywheres; leastways, I'll go my bottom cent, it ain't Peru. It was always a doubt if we could sell the schooner; I never rightly hoped to, and now I'm sure she ain't worth a hill of beans; what's wrong with her, I don't know; I only know it's something, or she wouldn't be here with this truck in her inside. Then again, if we lose her, and land in Peru, where are we? We can't declare the loss, or how did we get to Peru? In that case the merchant can't touch the insurance; most likely he'll go bust; and don't you think you see the three of us on the beach of Callao?'*

'There's no extradition there,' said Herrick.

'Well, my son, and we want to be extraded,' said the captain. 'What's our point? We want to have a consul extrade us as far as San Francisco and that merchant's office door. My idea is that Samoa would be found an eligible business centre. It's dead before the wind; the States have a consul there, and 'Frisco steamers call, so's we could skip right back and interview the merchant.'

'Samoa?' said Herrick. 'It will take us for ever to get there.'

'Oh, with a fair wind!' said the captain.

'No trouble about the log, eh?' asked Huish.

'No, *sir*,' said Davis. '*Light airs and baffling winds. Squalls and calms. D. R.: five miles. No obs. Pumps attended.* And fill in the barometer and thermometer off of last year's trip.' 'Never saw such a voyage,' says you to the consul. 'Thought I was going to run short ...' He stopped in mid career. ''Say,' he began again, and once more stopped. 'Beg your pardon, Herrick,' he added with undisguised humility, 'but did you keep the run of the stores?'

'Had I been told to do so, it should have been done, as the rest was done, to the best of my little ability,' said Herrick. 'As it was, the cook helped himself to what he pleased.'

Davis looked at the table.

'I drew it rather fine, you see,' he said at last. 'The great thing was to clear right out of Papeete before the consul could think better of it. Tell you what: I guess I'll take stock.'

And he rose from table and disappeared with a lamp in the lazarette.*

''Ere's another screw loose,' observed Huish.

'My man,' said Herrick, with a sudden gleam of animosity, 'it is still your watch on deck, and surely your wheel also?'

'You come the 'eavy swell, don't you, ducky?' said Huish.

'Stand away from that binnacle. Surely your w'eel, my man. Yah.'

He lit a cigar ostentatiously, and strolled into the waist with his hands in his pockets.

In a surprisingly short time, the captain reappeared; he did not look at Herrick, but called Huish back and sat down.

'Well,' he began, 'I've taken stock – roughly.' He paused as if for somebody to help him out; and none doing so, both gazing on him instead with manifest anxiety, he yet more heavily resumed. 'Well, it won't fight. We can't do it; that's the bed rock. I'm as sorry as what you can be, and sorrier. We can't look near Samoa. I don't know as we could get to Peru.'

'Wot-ju mean?' asked Huish brutally.

'I can't 'most tell myself,' replied the captain. 'I drew it fine; I said I did; but what's been going on here gets me! Appears as if the devil had been around. That cook must be the holiest kind of fraud. Only twelve days, too! Seems like craziness. I'll own up square to one thing: I seem to have figured too fine upon the flour. But the rest – my land! I'll never understand it! There's been more waste on this twopenny ship than what there is to an Atlantic Liner.' He stole a glance at his companions; nothing good was to be gleaned from their dark faces; and he had recourse to rage. 'You wait till I interview that cook!' he roared and smote the table with his fist. 'I'll interview the son of a gun so's he's never been spoken to before. I'll put a bead upon the—'

'You will not lay a finger on the man,' said Herrick. 'The fault is yours and you know it. If you turn a savage loose in your store-room, you know what to expect. I will not allow the man to be molested.'

It is hard to say how Davis might have taken this defiance; but he was diverted to a fresh assailant.

'Well!' drawled Huish, 'you're a plummy captain, ain't you? You're a blooming captain! Don't you set up any of your chat to me, John Dyvis: I know you now, you ain't any more use than a bloomin' dawl! Oh, you "don't know", don't you? Oh, it "gets you", do it? Oh, I dessay! W'y, we en't you 'owling for fresh tins every blessed day? 'Ow often 'ave I 'eard you send the 'ole bloomin' dinner off and tell the man to chuck it in the swill tub? And breakfast? Oh, my crikey! breakfast for ten, and you 'ollerin' for more! And now you "can't 'most tell"! Blow me, if it ain't enough to make a man write an insultin' letter to Gawd! You dror it mild, John Dyvis; don't 'andle me; I'm dyngerous.'

Davis sat like one bemused; it might even have been doubted if he heard, but the voice of the clerk rang about the cabin like that of a cormorant among the ledges of the cliff.

'That will do, Huish,' said Herrick.

'Oh, so you tyke his part, do you? you stuck-up sneerin' snob! Tyke it then. Come on, the pair of you. But as for John Dyvis, let him look out! He struck me the first night aboard, and I never took a blow yet but wot I gave as good. Let him knuckle down on his marrow bones and beg my pardon. That's my last word.'

'I stand by the Captain,' said Herrick. 'That makes us two to one, both good men; and the crew will all follow me. I hope I shall die very soon; but I have not the least objection to killing you before I go. I should prefer it so; I should do it with no more remorse than winking. Take care – take care, you little cad!'

The animosity with which these words were uttered was so marked in itself, and so remarkable in the man who uttered them that Huish stared, and even the humiliated Davis reared up his head and gazed at his defender. As for Herrick, the successive agitations and disappointments of the day had left him wholly reckless; he was conscious of a pleasant glow, an agreeable excitement; his head seemed empty, his eyeballs burned as he turned them, his throat was dry as a biscuit; the least dangerous man by nature, except in so far as the weak are always dangerous, at that moment he was ready to slay or to be slain with equal unconcern.

Here at least was the gage thrown down, and battle offered; he who should speak next would bring the matter to an issue there and then; all knew it to be so and hung back; and for many seconds by the cabin clock, the trio sat motionless and silent.

Then came an interruption, welcome as the flowers in May.

'Land ho!' sang out a voice on deck. 'Land a weatha bow!'

'Land!' cried Davis, springing to his feet. 'What's this? There ain't no land here.'

And as men may run from the chamber of a murdered corpse, the three ran forth out of the house and left their quarrel behind them, undecided.

The sky shaded down at the sea level to the white of opals; the sea itself, insolently, inkily blue, drew all about them the uncompromising wheel of the horizon. Search it as they pleased, not even the practised eye of Captain Davis could descry the smallest interruption. A few filmy clouds were slowly melting overhead; and about the schooner, as around the only point of interest, a tropic bird, white as a snowflake, hung, and circled, and displayed, as it turned, the long vermilion feather of its tail. Save the sea and the heaven, that was all.

'Who sang out land?' asked Davis. 'If there's any boy playing funny dog with me, I'll teach him skylarking!'

But Uncle Ned contentedly pointed to a part of the horizon, where a greenish, filmy iridescence could be discerned floating like smoke on the pale heavens.

Davis applied his glass to it, and then looked at the Kanaka. 'Call that land?' said he. 'Well, it's more than I do.'

'One time long ago,' said Uncle Ned, 'I see Anaa all-e-same that, four five hours befo' we come up. Capena he say sun go down, sun go up again; he say lagoon all-e-same milla.'

'All-e-same *what*?' asked Davis.

'Milla, sah,' said Uncle Ned.

'Oh, ah! mirror,' said Davis. 'I see; reflection from the lagoon. Well, you know, it is just possible, though it's strange I never heard of it. Here, let's look at the chart.'

They went back to the cabin, and found the position of the schooner well to windward of the archipelago in the midst of a white field of paper.

'There! you see for yourselves,' said Davis.

'And yet I don't know,' said Herrick, 'I somehow think there's something in it. I'll tell you one thing too, captain; that's all right about the reflection; I heard it in Papeete.'

'Fetch up that Findlay,* then!' said Davis. 'I'll try it all ways. An island wouldn't come amiss, the way we're fixed.'

The bulky volume was handed up to him, broken-backed as is the way with Findlay; and he turned to the place and began to run over the text, muttering to himself and turning over the pages with a wetted finger.

'Hullo!' he exclaimed. 'How's this?' And he read aloud. '*New Island*. According to M. Delille this island, which from private interests would remain unknown, lies, it is said, in lat. 12° 49′ 10″ S. long. 133° 6′ W. In addition to the position above given Commander Matthews, H.M.S. *Scorpion*, states that an island exists in lat. 12° 0′ S. long. 133° 16′ W. This must be the same, if such an island exists, which is very doubtful, and totally disbelieved in by South Sea traders.'

'Golly!' said Huish.

'It's rather in the conditional mood,' said Herrick.

'It's anything you please,' cried Davis, 'only there it is! That's our place, and don't you make any mistake.'

'"Which from private interests would remain unknown,"' read Herrick, over his shoulder. 'What may that mean?'

'It should mean pearls,' said Davis. 'A pearling island the government don't know about? That sounds like real estate. Or suppose it don't mean anything. Suppose it's just an island; I guess we could fill up with fish, and cocoanuts, and native stuff, and carry out the Samoa scheme hand over fist. How long did he say it was before they raised Anaa? Five hours, I think?'

'Four or five,' said Herrick.

Davis stepped to the door. 'What breeze had you that time you made Anaa, Uncle Ned?' said he.

'Six or seven knots,' was the reply.

'Thirty or thirty-five miles,' said Davis. 'High time we were shortening sail, then. If it is an island, we don't want to be butting our head against it in the dark; and if it isn't an island, we can get through it just as well by daylight. Ready about!' he roared.

And the schooner's head was laid for that elusive glimmer in the sky, which began already to pale in lustre and diminish in size, as the stain of breath vanishes from a window pane. At the same time she was reefed close down.

Part II
THE QUARTETTE

Chapter 7

THE PEARL-FISHER

About four in the morning, as the captain and Herrick sat together on the rail, there arose from the midst of the night in front of them the voice of breakers. Each sprang to his feet and stared and listened. The sound was continuous, like the passing of a train; no rise or fall could be distinguished; minute by minute the ocean heaved with an equal potency against the invisible isle; and as time passed, and Herrick waited in vain for any vicissitude in the volume of that roaring, a sense of the eternal weighed upon his mind. To the expert eye the isle itself was to be inferred from a certain string of blots along the starry heaven. And the schooner was laid to and anxiously observed till daylight.

There was little or no morning bank. A brightening came in the east; then a wash of some ineffable, faint, nameless hue between crimson and silver; and then coals of fire. These glimmered a while on the sea line, and seemed to brighten and darken and spread out, and still the night and the stars reigned undisturbed; it was as though a spark should catch and glow and creep along the foot of some heavy and almost incombustible wall-hanging, and the room itself be scarce menaced. Yet a little after, and the whole east glowed with gold and scarlet, and the hollow of heaven was filled with the daylight.

The isle – the undiscovered, the scarce believed-in – now lay before them and close aboard; and Herrick thought that never in his dreams had he beheld anything more strange and delicate. The beach was excellently white, the continuous barrier of trees inimitably green; the land perhaps ten feet high, the trees thirty more. Every here and there, as the schooner coasted northward, the wood was intermitted; and he could see clear over the inconsiderable strip of land (as a man looks over a wall) to the lagoon within – and clear over that again to where the far side of the atoll prolonged its pencilling of trees against the morning sky. He tortured himself to find analogies. The isle was like the rim of a great vessel sunken in the waters; it was like the embankment of an annular railway grown upon with wood: so slender it seemed amidst the outrageous breakers, so frail and pretty, he would scarce have wondered to see it sink and disappear without a sound, and the waves close smoothly over its descent.

Meanwhile the captain was in the forecross-trees, glass in hand, his eyes in every quarter, spying for an entrance, spying for signs of tenancy. But the isle continued to unfold itself in joints, and to run out in indeterminate capes, and still there was neither house nor man, nor the smoke of fire. Here a multitude of sea-birds soared and twinkled, and fished in the blue waters; and there, and for miles together, the fringe of cocoa-palm and pandanus extended desolate, and made desirable green bowers for nobody to visit, and the silence of death was only broken by the throbbing of the sea.

The airs were very light, their speed was small; the heat intense. The decks were scorching underfoot, the sun flamed overhead, brazen, out of a brazen sky; the pitch bubbled in the seams, and the brains in the brain-pan. And all the while the excitement of the three adventurers glowed about their bones like a fever. They whispered, and nodded, and pointed, and put mouth to ear, with a singular instinct of secrecy, approaching that island underhand like eavesdroppers and thieves; and even Davis from the cross-trees gave his orders mostly by gestures. The hands shared in this mute strain, like dogs, without comprehending it; and through the roar of so many miles of breakers, it was a silent ship that approached an empty island.

At last they drew near to the break in that interminable gangway. A spur of coral sand stood forth on the one hand; on the other a high and thick tuft of trees cut off the view; between was the mouth of the huge laver. Twice a day the ocean crowded in that narrow entrance and was heaped between these frail walls; twice a day, with the return of the ebb, the mighty surplusage of water must struggle to escape. The hour in which the *Farallone* came there was the hour of flood. The sea turned (as with the instinct of the homing pigeon) for the vast receptacle, swept eddying through the gates, was transmuted, as it did so, into a wonder of watery and silken hues, and brimmed into the inland sea beyond. The schooner looked up close-hauled, and was caught and carried away by the influx like a toy. She skimmed; she flew; a momentary shadow touched her decks from the shore-side trees; the bottom of the channel showed up for a moment and was in a moment gone; the next, she floated on the bosom of the lagoon, and below, in the transparent chamber of waters, a myriad of many-coloured fishes were sporting, a myriad pale flowers of coral diversified the floor.

Herrick stood transported. In the gratified lust of his eye, he forgot the past and the present; forgot that he was menaced by a prison on the one hand and starvation on the other; forgot that he was come to that island, desperately foraging, clutching at expedients. A drove of fishes, painted like the rainbow and billed like parrots, hovered up in the shadow of the schooner, and passed clear of it, and glinted in the submarine sun. They were beautiful, like birds, and their silent passage impressed him like a strain of song.

Meanwhile, to the eye of Davis in the cross-trees, the lagoon continued to expand its empty waters, and the long succession of the shore-side trees to be paid out like fishing line off a reel. And still there was no mark of habitation. The schooner, immediately on entering, had been kept away to the nor'ard where the water seemed to be the most deep; and she was now skimming past the tall grove of trees, which stood on that side of the channel and denied further view. Of the whole of the low shores of the island, only this bight remained to be revealed. And suddenly the curtain was raised; they began to open out a haven, snugly elbowed there, and beheld, with an astonishment beyond words, the roofs of men.

The appearance, thus 'instantaneously disclosed' to those on the deck of the *Farallone*, was not that of a city, rather of a substantial country farm with its attendant hamlet: a long line of sheds and store-houses; apart, upon the one side, a deep-verandah'ed dwelling-house; on the other, perhaps a dozen native huts; a building with a belfry and some rude offer at architectural features that might be thought to mark it out for a chapel; on the beach in front some heavy boats drawn up, and a pile of timber running forth into the burning shallows of the lagoon. From a flagstaff at the pierhead, the red ensign of England was displayed. Behind, about, and over, the same tall grove of palms, which had masked the settlement in the beginning, prolonged its roof of tumultuous green fans, and turned and ruffled overhead, and sang its silver song all day in the wind. The place had the indescribable but unmistakable appearance of being in commission; yet there breathed from it a sense of desertion that was almost poignant, no human figure was to be observed going to and fro about the houses, and there was no sound of human industry or enjoyment. Only, on the top of the beach and hard by the flagstaff, a woman of exorbitant stature and as white as snow was to be seen beckoning with uplifted arm. The second glance identified her as a piece of naval sculpture, the figure-head of a ship that had long hovered and plunged into so many running billows, and was now brought ashore to be the ensign and presiding genius of that empty town.

The *Farallone* made a soldier's breeze of it; the wind, besides, was stronger inside than without under the lee of the land; and the stolen schooner opened out successive objects with the swiftness of a panorama, so that the adventurers stood speechless. The flag spoke for itself; it was no frayed and weathered trophy that had beaten itself to pieces on the post, flying over desolation; and to make assurance stronger, there was to be descried in the deep shade of the verandah, a glitter of crystal and the fluttering of white napery. If the figure-head at the pier end, with its perpetual gesture and its leprous whiteness, reigned alone in that hamlet as it seemed to do, it would not have reigned long. Men's hands had been busy, men's feet stirring there, within the circuit of the clock. The *Farallones* were sure of it; their eyes dug in the deep shadow of the palms for some one hiding; if intensity of looking might have prevailed, they would have pierced the walls of houses; and there came to them, in these pregnant seconds, a sense of being watched and played with, and of a blow impending, that was hardly bearable.

The extreme point of palms they had just passed enclosed a creek, which was thus hidden up to the last moment from the eyes of those on board; and from this, a boat put suddenly and briskly out, and a voice hailed.

'Schooner ahoy!' it cried. 'Stand in for the pier! In two cables' lengths you'll have twenty fathoms water and good holding ground.'

The boat was manned with a couple of brown oarsmen in scanty kilts of blue. The speaker, who was steering, wore white clothes, the full dress of the tropics; a wide hat shaded his face; but it could be seen that he was of stalwart size, and his voice sounded like a gentleman's. So much could be made out. It was plain, besides, that the *Farallone* had been descried some time before at sea, and the inhabitants were prepared for its reception.

Mechanically the orders were obeyed, and the ship berthed; and the three adventurers gathered aft beside the house and waited, with galloping pulses and a perfect vacancy of mind, the coming of the stranger who might mean so much to them. They had no plan, no story prepared; there was no time to make one; they were caught red-handed and must stand their chance. Yet this anxiety was chequered with hope. The island being undeclared, it was not possible the man could hold any office or be in a position to demand their papers. And beyond that, if there was any truth in Findlay, as it now seemed there should be, he was the representative of the 'private reasons,' he must see their coming with a profound disappointment; and perhaps (hope whispered) he would be willing and able to purchase their silence.

The boat was by that time forging alongside, and they were able at last to see what manner of man they had to do with. He was a huge fellow, six feet four in height, and of a build proportionately strong, but his sinews seemed to be dissolved in a listlessness that was more than languor. It was only the eye that corrected this impression; an eye of an unusual mingled brilliancy and softness, sombre as coal and with lights that outshone the topaz; an eye of unimpaired health and virility; an eye that bid you beware of the man's devastating anger. A complexion, naturally dark, had been tanned in the island to a hue hardly distinguishable from that of a Tahitian; only his manners and movements, and the living force that dwelt in him, like fire in flint, betrayed the European. He was dressed in white drill, exquisitely made; his scarf and tie were of tender-coloured silks; on the thwart beside him there leaned a Winchester rifle.

'Is the doctor on board?' he cried as he came up. 'Dr Symonds, I mean? You never heard of him? Nor yet of the *Trinity Hall*? Ah!'

He did not look surprised, seemed rather to affect it in politeness; but his eye rested on each of the three white men in succession with a sudden weight of curiosity that was almost savage. 'Ah, *then*!' said he, 'there is some small mistake, no doubt, and I must ask you to what I am indebted for this pleasure?'

He was by this time on the deck, but he had the art to be quite unapproachable; the friendliest vulgarian, three parts drunk, would have known better than take liberties; and not one of the adventurers so much as offered to shake hands.

'Well,' said Davis, 'I suppose you may call it an accident. We had heard of your island, and read that thing in the Directory about the *private reasons*, you see; so when we saw the lagoon reflected in the sky, we put her head for it at once, and so here we are.'

''Ope we don't intrude!' said Huish.

The stranger looked at Huish with an air of faint surprise, and looked pointedly away again. It was hard to be more offensive in dumb show.

'It may suit me, your coming here,' he said. 'My own schooner is overdue, and I may put something in your way in the meantime. Are you open to a charter?'

'Well, I guess so,' said Davis; 'it depends.'

'My name is Attwater,' continued the stranger. 'You, I presume, are the captain?'

'Yes, sir. I am the captain of this ship: Captain Brown,' was the reply.

'Well, see 'ere!' said Huish, 'better begin fair! 'E's skipper on deck right enough, but not below. Below, we're all equal, all got a lay in the adventure; when it comes to business, I'm as good as 'e; and what I say is, let's go into the 'ouse and have a lush, and talk it over among pals. We've some prime fizz,' he said, and winked.

The presence of the gentleman lighted up like a candle the vulgarity of the clerk; and Herrick instinctively, as one shields himself from pain, made haste to interrupt.

'My name is Hay,' said he, 'since introductions are going. We shall be very glad if you will step inside.'

Attwater leaned to him swiftly. 'University man?' said he.

'Yes, Merton,' said Herrick, and the next moment blushed scarlet at his indiscretion.

'I am of the other lot,' said Attwater: 'Trinity Hall, Cambridge. I called my schooner after the old shop. Well! this is a queer place and company for us to meet in, Mr Hay,' he pursued, with easy incivility to the others. 'But do you bear out ... I beg this gentleman's pardon, I really did not catch his name.'

'My name is 'Uish, sir,' returned the clerk, and blushed in turn.

'Ah!' said Attwater. And then turning again to Herrick, 'Do you bear out Mr Whish's description of your vintage? or was it only the unaffected poetry of his own nature bubbling up?'

Herrick was embarrassed; the silken brutality of their visitor made him blush; that he should be accepted as an equal, and the others thus pointedly ignored, pleased him in spite of himself, and then ran through his veins in a recoil of anger.

'I don't know,' he said. 'It's only California; it's good enough, I believe.'

Attwater seemed to make up his mind. 'Well then, I'll tell you what: you three gentlemen come ashore this evening and bring

a basket of wine with you; I'll try and find the food,' he said.
'And by the by, here is a question I should have asked you when
I come on board: have you had smallpox?'

'Personally, no,' said Herrick. 'But the schooner had it.'

'Deaths?' from Attwater.

'Two,' said Herrick.

'Well, it is a dreadful sickness,' said Attwater.

''Ad you any deaths?' asked Huish, ''ere on the island?'

'Twenty-nine,' said Attwater. 'Twenty-nine deaths and thirty-
one cases, out of thirty-three souls upon the island. – That's a
strange way to calculate, Mr Hay, is it not? Souls! I never say it
but it startles me.'

'Oh, so that's why everything's deserted?' said Huish.

'That is why, Mr Whish,' said Attwater; 'that is why the
house is empty and the graveyard full.'

'Twenty-nine out of thirty-three!' exclaimed Herrick, 'Why,
when it came to burying – or did you bother burying?'

'Scarcely,' said Attwater; 'or there was one day at least when
we gave up. There were five of the dead that morning, and
thirteen of the dying, and no one able to go about except the
sexton and myself. We held a council of war, took the . . . empty
bottles . . . into the lagoon, and . . . buried them.' He looked
over his shoulder, back at the bright water. 'Well, so you'll
come to dinner, then? Shall we say half-past six. *So* good of
you!'

His voice, in uttering these conventional phrases, fell at once
into the false measure of society; and Herrick unconsciously
followed the example.

'I am sure we shall be very glad,' he said. 'At half-past six?
Thank you so very much.'

> ' "For my voice has been tuned to the note of the gun
>   That startles the deep when the combat's begun," '*

quoted Attwater, with a smile, which instantly gave way to an
air of funereal solemnity. 'I shall particularly expect Mr Whish,'
he continued. 'Mr Whish, I trust you understand the invitation?'

'I believe you, my boy!' replied the genial Huish.

'That is right then; and quite understood, is it not?' said Attwater. 'Mr Whish and Captain Brown at six-thirty without fault – and you, Hay, at four sharp.'

And he called his boat.

During all this talk, a load of thought or anxiety had weighed upon the captain. There was no part for which nature had so liberally endowed him as that of the genial ship captain. But today he was silent and abstracted. Those who knew him could see that he hearkened close to every syllable, and seemed to ponder and try it in balances. It would have been hard to say what look there was, cold, attentive, and sinister, as of a man maturing plans, which still brooded over the unconscious guest; it was here, it was there, it was nowhere; it was now so little that Herrick chid himself for an idle fancy; and anon it was so gross and palpable that you could say every hair on the man's head talked mischief.

He woke up now, as with a start. 'You were talking of a charter,' said he.

'Was I?' said Attwater. 'Well, let's talk of it no more at present.'

'Your own schooner is overdue, I understand?' continued the captain.

'You understand perfectly, Captain Brown,' said Attwater; 'thirty-three days overdue at noon today.'

'She comes and goes, eh? plies between here and . . . ?' hinted the captain.

'Exactly; every four months; three trips in the year,' said Attwater.

'You go in her, ever?' asked Davis.

'No, one stops here,' said Attwater, 'one has plenty to attend to.'

'Stop here, do you?' cried Davis. 'Say, how long?'

'How long, O Lord,' said Attwater with perfect, stern gravity. 'But it does not seem so,' he added, with a smile.

'No, I dare say not,' said Davis. 'No, I suppose not. Not with all your gods about you, and in as snug a berth as this. For it is a pretty snug berth,' said he, with a sweeping look.

'The spot, as you are good enough to indicate, is not entirely intolerable,' was the reply.

'Shell, I suppose?' said Davis.

'Yes, there was shell,' said Attwater.

'This is a considerable big beast of a lagoon, sir,' said the captain. 'Was there a – was the fishing – would you call the fishing anyways *good*?'

'I don't know that I would call it anyways anything,' said Attwater, 'if you put it to me direct.'

'There were pearls too?' said Davis.

'Pearls, too,' said Attwater.

'Well, I give out!' laughed Davis, and his laughter rang cracked like a false piece. 'If you're not going to tell, you're not going to tell, and there's an end to it.'

'There can be no reason why I should affect the least degree of secrecy about my island,' returned Attwater; 'that came wholly to an end with your arrival; and I am sure, at any rate, that gentlemen like you and Mr Whish, I should have always been charmed to make perfectly at home. The point on which we are now differing – if you can call it a difference – is one of times and seasons. I have some information which you think I might impart, and I think not. Well, we'll see tonight! By-by, Whish!' He stepped into his boat and shoved off. 'All understood, then?' said he. 'The captain and Mr Whish at six-thirty, and you, Hay, at four precise. You understand that, Hay? Mind, I take no denial. If you're not there by the time named, there will be no banquet; no song, no supper, Mr Whish!'

White birds whisked in the air above, a shoal of parti-coloured fishes in the scarce denser medium below; between, like Mahomet's coffin, the boat drew away briskly on the surface, and its shadow followed it over the glittering floor of the lagoon. Attwater looked steadily back over his shoulders as he sat; he did not once remove his eyes from the *Farallone* and the group on her quarter-deck beside the house, till his boat ground upon the pier. Thence, with an agile pace, he hurried ashore, and they saw his white clothes shining in the chequered dusk of the grove until the house received him.

The captain, with a gesture and a speaking countenance, called the adventurers into the cabin.

'Well,' he said to Herrick, when they were seated, 'there's one good job at least. He's taken to you in earnest.'

'Why should that be a good job?' said Herrick.

'Oh, you'll see how it pans out presently,' returned Davis. 'You go ashore and stand in with him, that's all! You'll get lots of pointers; you can find out what he has, and what the charter is, and who's the fourth man – for there's four of them, and we're only three.'

'And suppose I do, what next?' cried Herrick. 'Answer me that!'

'So I will, Robert Herrick,' said the captain. 'But first, let's see all clear. I guess you know,' he said with an imperious solemnity, 'I guess you know the bottom is out of this *Farallone* speculation? I guess you know it's *right* out? and if this old island hadn't been turned up right when it did, I guess you know where you and I and Huish would have been?'

'Yes, I know that,' said Herrick. 'No matter who's to blame, I know it. And what next?'

'No matter who's to blame, you know it, right enough,' said the captain, 'and I'm obliged to you for the reminder. Now here's this Attwater: what do you think of him?'

'I do not know,' said Herrick. 'I am attracted and repelled. He was insufferably rude to you.'

'And you, Huish?' said the captain.

Huish sat cleaning a favourite briar root; he scarce looked up from that engrossing task. 'Don't ast me what I think of him!' he said. 'There's a day comin', I pray Gawd, when I can tell it him myself.'

'Huish means the same as what I do,' said Davis. 'When that man came stepping around, and saying "Look here, I'm Attwater" – and you knew it was so, by God! – I sized him right straight up. Here's the real article, I said, and I don't like it; here's the real, first-rate, copper-bottomed aristocrat. '*Aw! don't know ye, do I? God damn ye, did God make ye?*' No, that couldn't be nothing but genuine; a man got to be born to that, and notice! smart as champagne and hard as nails; no kind of a fool; no, *sir*! not a pound of him! Well, what's he here upon this beastly island for? I said. *He's* not here collecting eggs. He's a palace at home, and powdered flunkies; and if he don't stay there, you bet he knows the reason why! Follow?'

'O yes, I 'ear you,' said Huish.

'He's been doing good business here, then,' continued the captain. 'For ten years, he's been doing a great business. It's pearl and shell, of course; there couldn't be nothing else in such a place, and no doubt the shell goes off regularly by this *Trinity Hall*, and the money for it straight into the bank, so that's no use to us. But what else is there? Is there nothing else he would be likely to keep here? Is there nothing else he would be bound to keep here? Yes, sir; the pearls! First, because they're too valuable to trust out of his hands. Second, because pearls want a lot of handling and matching; and the man who sells his pearls as they come in, one here, one there, instead of hanging back and holding up – well, that man's a fool, and it's not Attwater.'

'Likely,' said Huish, 'that's w'at it is; not proved, but likely.'

'It's proved,' said Davis bluntly.

'Suppose it was?' said Herrick. 'Suppose that was all so, and he had these pearls – a ten years' collection of them? – Suppose he had? There's my question.'

The captain drummed with his thick hands on the board in front of him; he looked steadily in Herrick's face, and Herrick as steadily looked upon the table and the pattering fingers; there was a gentle oscillation of the anchored ship, and a big patch of sunlight travelled to and fro between the one and the other.

'Hear me!' Herrick burst out suddenly.

'No, you better hear me first,' said Davis. 'Hear me and understand me. *We've* got no use for that fellow, whatever you may have. He's your kind, he's not ours; he's took to you, and he's wiped his boots on me and Huish. Save him if you can!'

'Save him?' repeated Herrick.

'Save him, if you're able!' reiterated Davis, with a blow of his clenched fist. 'Go ashore, and talk him smooth; and if you get him and his pearls aboard, I'll spare him. If you don't, there's going to be a funeral. Is that so, Huish? does that suit you?'

'I ain't a forgiving man,' said Huish, 'but I'm not the sort to spoil business neither. Bring the bloke on board and bring his pearls along with him, and you can have it your own way; maroon him where you like – I'm agreeable.'

'Well, and if I can't?' cried Herrick, while the sweat streamed upon his face. 'You talk to me as if I was God Almighty, to do this and that! But if I can't?'

'My son,' said the captain, 'you better do your level best, or you'll see sights!'

'O yes,' said Huish. 'O crikey, yes!' He looked across at Herrick with a toothless smile that was shocking in its savagery; and his ear caught apparently by the trivial expression he had used, broke into a piece of the chorus of a comic song which he must have heard twenty years before in London: meaningless gibberish that, in that hour and place, seemed hateful as a blasphemy: 'Hikey, pikey, crikey, fikey, chillingawallaba dory.'

The captain suffered him to finish; his face was unchanged.

'The way things are, there's many a man that wouldn't let you go ashore,' he resumed. 'But I'm not that kind. I know you'd never go back on me, Herrick! Or if you choose to – go, and do it, and be damned!' he cried, and rose abruptly from the table.

He walked out of the house; and as he reached the door, turned and called Huish, suddenly and violently, like the barking of a dog. Huish followed, and Herrick remained alone in the cabin.

'Now, see here!' whispered Davis. 'I know that man. If you open your mouth to him again, you'll ruin all.'

Chapter 8

BETTER ACQUAINTANCE

The boat was gone again, and already half-way to the *Farallone*, before Herrick turned and went unwillingly up the pier. From the crown of the beach, the figure-head confronted him with what seemed irony, her helmeted head tossed back, her formidable arm apparently hurling something, whether shell or missile, in the direction of the anchored schooner. She seemed a defiant deity from the island, coming forth to its threshold with a rush as of one about to fly, and perpetuated in that dashing attitude. Herrick looked up at her, where she towered above him head and shoulders, with singular feelings of curiosity and romance, and suffered his mind to travel to and fro in her life-history. So long she had been the blind conductress of a ship among the waves; so long she had stood here idle in the violent sun, that yet did not avail to blister her; and was even this the end of so many adventures? he wondered, or was more behind? And he could have found in his heart to regret that she was not a goddess, nor yet he a pagan, that he might have bowed down before her in that hour of difficulty.

When he now went forward, it was cool with the shadow of many well-grown palms; draughts of the dying breeze swung them together overhead; and on all sides, with a swiftness beyond dragon-flies or swallows, the spots of sunshine flitted, and hovered, and returned. Underfoot, the sand was fairly solid and quite level, and Herrick's steps fell there noiseless as in new-fallen snow. It bore the marks of having been once weeded like a garden alley at home; but the pestilence had done its work, and the weeds were returning. The buildings of the settlement showed here and there through the stems of the colonnade, fresh painted, trim and dandy, and all silent as the grave. Only, here and there in the crypt, there was a rustle and scurry and some crowing of poultry; and from behind the house with the verandahs, he saw smoke arise and heard the crackling of a fire.

The stone houses were nearest him upon his right. The first was locked; in the second, he could dimly perceive, through a window, a certain accumulation of pearl-shell piled in the far end; the third, which stood gaping open on the afternoon, seized on the mind of Herrick with its multiplicity and disorder of romantic things. Therein were cables, windlasses and blocks of every size and capacity; cabin windows and ladders; rusty tanks, a companion hutch; a binnacle with its brass mountings and its compass idly pointing, in the confusion and dusk of that shed, to a forgotten pole; ropes, anchors, harpoons, a blubber dipper of copper, green with years, a steering wheel, a tool chest with the vessel's name upon the top, the *Asia*: a whole curiosity-shop of sea curios, gross and solid, heavy to lift, ill to break, bound with brass and shod with iron. Two wrecks at the least must have contributed to this random heap of lumber; and as Herrick looked upon it, it seemed to him as if the two ships' companies were there on guard, and he heard the tread of feet and whisperings, and saw with the tail of his eye the commonplace ghosts of sailor men.

This was not merely the work of an aroused imagination, but had something sensible to go upon; sounds of a stealthy approach were no doubt audible; and while he still stood staring at the lumber, the voice of his host sounded suddenly, and with even more than the customary softness of enunciation, from behind.

'Junk,' it said, 'only old junk! And does Mr Hay find a parable?'

'I find at least a strong impression,' replied Herrick, turning quickly, lest he might be able to catch, on the face of the speaker, some commentary on the words.

Attwater stood in the doorway, which he almost wholly filled; his hands stretched above his head and grasping the architrave. He smiled when their eyes met, but the expression was inscrutable.

'Yes, a powerful impression. You are like me; nothing so affecting as ships!' said he. 'The ruins of an empire would leave me frigid, when a bit of an old rail that an old shellback leaned on in the middle watch, would bring me up all standing. But come, let's see some more of the island. It's all sand and coral and palm trees; but there's a kind of a quaintness in the place.'

'I find it heavenly,' said Herrick, breathing deep, with head bared in the shadow.

'Ah, that's because you're new from sea,' said Attwater. 'I dare say, too, you can appreciate what one calls it. It's a lovely name. It has a flavour, it has a colour, it has a ring and fall to it; it's like its author – it's half Christian! Remember your first view of the island, and how it's only woods and water; and suppose you had asked somebody for the name, and he had answered – *nemorosa Zacynthos*!'*

'*Jam medio apparet fluctu*!' exclaimed Herrick. 'Ye gods, yes, how good!'

'If it gets upon the chart, the skippers will make nice work of it,' said Attwater. 'But here, come and see the diving-shed.'

He opened a door, and Herrick saw a large display of apparatus neatly ordered: pumps and pipes, and the leaded boots, and the huge snouted helmets shining in rows along the wall; ten complete outfits.

'The whole eastern half of my lagoon is shallow, you must understand,' said Attwater; 'so we were able to get in the dress to great advantage. It paid beyond belief, and was a queer sight when they were at it, and these marine monsters' – tapping the nearest of the helmets – 'kept appearing and reappearing in the midst of the lagoon. Fond of parables?' he asked abruptly.

'O yes!' said Herrick.

'Well, I saw these machines come up dripping and go down again, and come up dripping and go down again, and all the while the fellow inside as dry as toast!' said Attwater; 'and I thought we all wanted a dress to go down into the world in, and come up scatheless. What do you think the name was?' he inquired.

'Self-conceit,' said Herrick.

'Ah, but I mean seriously!' said Attwater.

'Call it self-respect, then!' corrected Herrick, with a laugh.

'And why not Grace? Why not God's Grace, Hay?' asked Attwater. 'Why not the grace of your Maker and Redeemer, He who died for you, He who upholds you, He whom you daily crucify afresh? There is nothing here,' — striking on his bosom — 'nothing there' — smiting the wall — 'and nothing there' — stamping — 'nothing but God's Grace! We walk upon it, we breathe it; we live and die by it; it makes the nails and axles of the universe; and a puppy in pyjamas prefers self-conceit!' The huge dark man stood over against Herrick by the line of the divers' helmets, and seemed to swell and glow; and the next moment the life had gone from him. 'I beg your pardon,' said he; 'I see you don't believe in God?'

'Not in your sense, I am afraid,' said Herrick.

'I never argue with young atheists or habitual drunkards,' said Attwater flippantly. 'Let us go across the island to the outer beach.'

It was but a little way, the greatest width of that island scarce exceeding a furlong, and they walked gently. Herrick was like one in a dream. He had come there with a mind divided; come prepared to study that ambiguous and sneering mask, drag out the essential man from underneath, and act accordingly; decision being till then postponed. Iron cruelty, an iron insensibility to the suffering of others, the uncompromising pursuit of his own interests, cold culture, manners without humanity; these he had looked for, these he still thought he saw. But to find the whole machine thus glow with the reverberation of religious zeal, surprised him beyond words; and he laboured in vain, as he walked, to piece together into any kind of whole his odds and ends of knowledge — to adjust again into any kind of focus with itself, his picture of the man beside him.

'What brought you here to the South Seas?' he asked presently.

'Many things,' said Attwater. 'Youth, curiosity, romance, the love of the sea, and (it will surprise you to hear) an interest in missions. That has a good deal declined, which will surprise you less. They go the wrong way to work; they are too parsonish, too much of the old wife, and even the old apple wife. *Clothes, clothes*, are their idea; but clothes are not Christianity, any more than they are the sun in heaven, or could take the place of it! They think a parsonage with roses, and church bells, and nice old women bobbing in the lanes, are part and parcel of religion. But religion is a savage thing, like the universe it illuminates; savage, cold, and bare, but infinitely strong.'

'And you found this island by an accident?' said Herrick.

'As you did!' said Attwater. 'And since then I have had a business, and a colony, and a mission of my own. I was a man of the world before I was a Christian; I'm a man of the world still, and I made my mission pay. No good ever came of coddling. A man has to stand up in God's sight and work up to his weight avoirdupois; then I'll talk to him, but not before. I gave these beggars what they wanted: a judge in Israel, the bearer of the sword and scourge; I was making a new people here; and behold, the angel of the Lord smote them and they were not!'

With the very uttering of the words, which were accompanied by a gesture, they came forth out of the porch of the palm wood by the margin of the sea and full in front of the sun which was near setting. Before them the surf broke slowly. All around, with an air of imperfect wooden things inspired with wicked activity, the crabs trundled and scuttled into holes. On the right, whither Attwater pointed and abruptly turned, was the cemetery of the island, a field of broken stones from the bigness of a child's hand to that of his head, diversified by many mounds of the same material, and walled by a rude rectangular enclosure. Nothing grew there but a shrub or two with some white flowers; nothing but the number of the mounds, and their disquieting shape, indicated the presence of the dead.

'The rude forefathers of the hamlet sleep!'

quoted Attwater as he entered by the open gateway into that unholy close. 'Coral to coral, pebbles to pebbles,' he said, 'this has been the main scene of my activity in the South Pacific. Some were good, and some bad, and the majority (of course and always) null. Here was a fellow, now, that used to frisk like a dog; if you had called him he came like an arrow from a bow; if you had not, and he came unbidden, you should have seen the deprecating eye and the little intricate dancing step. Well, his trouble is over now, he has lain down with kings and councillors; the rest of his acts, are they not written in the book of the chronicles? That fellow was from Penrhyn; like all the Penrhyn islanders he was ill to manage; heady, jealous, violent: the man with the nose! He lies here quiet enough. And so they all lie.

"And darkness was the burier of the dead!" '*

He stood, in the strong glow of the sunset, with bowed head; his voice sounded now sweet and now bitter with the varying sense.

'You loved these people?' cried Herrick, strangely touched.

'I?' said Attwater. 'Dear no! Don't think me a philanthropist. I dislike men, and hate women. If I like the islands at all, it is because you see them here plucked of their lendings, their dead birds and cocked hats, their petticoats and coloured hose. Here was one I liked though,' and he set his foot upon a mound. 'He was a fine savage fellow; he had a dark soul; yes, I liked this one. I am fanciful,' he added, looking hard at Herrick, 'and I take fads. I like you.'

Herrick turned swiftly and looked far away to where the clouds were beginning to troop together and amass themselves round the obsequies of day. 'No one can like me,' he said.

'You are wrong there,' said the other, 'as a man usually is about himself. You are attractive, very attractive.'

'It is not me,' said Herrick; 'no one can like me. If you knew how I despised myself – and why!' His voice rang out in the quiet graveyard.

'I knew that you despised yourself,' said Attwater. 'I saw the blood come into your face today when you remembered Oxford. And I could have blushed for you myself, to see a man, a gentleman, with these two vulgar wolves.'

Herrick faced him with a thrill. 'Wolves?' he repeated.

'I said wolves and vulgar wolves,' said Attwater. 'Do you know that today, when I came on board, I trembled?'

'You concealed it well,' stammered Herrick.

'A habit of mine,' said Attwater. 'But I was afraid, for all that: I was afraid of the two wolves.' He raised his hand slowly. 'And now, Hay, you poor lost puppy, what do you do with the two wolves?'

'What do I do? I don't do anything,' said Herrick. 'There is nothing wrong; all is above board; Captain Brown is a good soul; he is a . . . he is . . .' The phantom voice of Davis called in his ear: 'There's going to be a funeral' and the sweat burst forth and streamed on his brow. 'He is a family man,' he resumed again, swallowing; 'he has children at home – and a wife.'

'And a very nice man?' said Attwater. 'And so is Mr Whish, no doubt?'

'I won't go so far as that,' said Herrick. 'I do not like Huish. And yet . . . he has his merits too.'

'And, in short, take them for all in all, as good a ship's company as one would ask?' said Attwater.

'O yes,' said Herrick, 'quite.'

'So then we approach the other point of why you despise yourself?' said Attwater.

'Do we not all despise ourselves?' cried Herrick. 'Do not you?'

'Oh, I say I do. But do I?' said Attwater. 'One thing I know at least: I never gave a cry like yours. Hay! it came from a bad conscience! Ah, man, that poor diving dress of self-conceit is sadly tattered! Today, now, while the sun sets, and here in this burying place of brown innocents, fall on your knees and cast your sins and sorrows on the Redeemer. Hay—'

'Not Hay!' interrupted the other, strangling. 'Don't call

me that! I mean . . . For God's sake, can't you see I'm on the rack?'

'I see it, I know it, I put and keep you there, my fingers are on the screws!' said Attwater. 'Please God, I will bring a penitent this night before His throne. Come, come to the mercy-seat! He waits to be gracious, man — waits to be gracious!'

He spread out his arms like a crucifix, his face shone with the brightness of a seraph's; in his voice, as it rose to the last word, the tears seemed ready.

Herrick made a vigorous call upon himself. 'Attwater,' he said, 'you push me beyond bearing. What am I to do? I do not believe. It is living truth to you; to me, upon my conscience, only folk-lore. I do not believe there is any form of words under heaven by which I can lift the burthen from my shoulders. I must stagger on to the end with the pack of my responsibility; I cannot shift it; do you suppose I would not, if I thought I could? I cannot — cannot — cannot — and let that suffice.'

The rapture was all gone from Attwater's countenance; the dark apostle had disappeared; and in his place there stood an easy, sneering gentleman, who took off his hat and bowed. It was pertly done, and the blood burned in Herrick's face.

'What do you mean by that?' he cried.

'Well, shall we go back to the house?' said Attwater. 'Our guests will soon be due.'

Herrick stood his ground a moment with clenched fists and teeth; and as he so stood, the fact of his errand there slowly swung clear in front of him, like the moon out of clouds. He had come to lure that man on board; he was failing, even if it could be said that he had tried; he was sure to fail now, and knew it, and knew it was better so. And what was to be next?

With a groan he turned to follow his host, who was standing with polite smile, and instantly and somewhat obsequiously led the way in the now darkened colonnade of palms. There they went in silence, the earth gave up richly of her perfume, the air tasted warm and aromatic in the nostrils; and from a great way

forward in the wood, the brightness of lights and fire marked
out the house of Attwater.

Herrick meanwhile resolved and resisted an immense temptation to go up, to touch him on the arm and breathe a word in
his ear: 'Beware, they are going to murder you.' There would
be one life saved; but what of the two others? The three lives
went up and down before him like buckets in a well, or like
the scales of balances. It had come to a choice, and one that
must be speedy. For certain invaluable minutes, the wheels
of life ran before him, and he could still divert them with a
touch to the one side or the other, still choose who was to
live and who was to die. He considered the men. Attwater
intrigued, puzzled, dazzled, enchanted and revolted him; alive,
he seemed but a doubtful good; and the thought of him lying
dead was so unwelcome that it pursued him, like a vision, with
every circumstance of colour and sound. Incessantly, he had
before him the image of that great mass of man stricken down
in varying attitudes and with varying wounds; fallen prone,
fallen supine, fallen on his side; or clinging to a doorpost with
the changing face and the relaxing fingers of the death-agony.
He heard the click of the trigger, the thud of the ball, the cry
of the victim; he saw the blood flow. And this building up
of circumstance was like a consecration of the man, till he
seemed to walk in sacrificial fillets. Next he considered Davis,
with his thick-fingered, coarse-grained, oat-bread commonness
of nature, his indomitable valour and mirth in the old days
of their starvation, the endearing blend of his faults and
virtues, the sudden shining forth of a tenderness that lay too
deep for tears; his children, Adar and her bowel complaint, and
Adar's doll. No, death could not be suffered to approach that
head even in fancy; with a general heat and a bracing of his
muscles, it was borne in on Herrick that Adar's father would
find in him a son to the death. And even Huish showed a little
in that sacredness; by the tacit adoption of daily life they were
become brothers; there was an implied bond of loyalty in their
cohabitation of the ship and their passed miseries, to which
Herrick must be a little true or wholly dishonoured. Horror of

sudden death for horror of sudden death, there was here no hesitation possible: it must be Attwater. And no sooner was the thought formed (which was a sentence) than his whole mind of man ran in a panic to the other side: and when he looked within himself, he was aware only of turbulence and inarticulate outcry.

In all this there was no thought of Robert Herrick. He had complied with the ebb-tide in man's affairs, and the tide had carried him away; he heard already the roaring of the maelstrom that must hurry him under. And in his bedevilled and dis-honoured soul there was no thought of self.

For how long he walked silent by his companion Herrick had no guess. The clouds rolled suddenly away; the orgasm was over; he found himself placid with the placidity of despair; there returned to him the power of commonplace speech; and he heard with surprise his own voice say: 'What a lovely evening!'

'Is it not?' said Attwater. 'Yes, the evenings here would be very pleasant if one had anything to do. By day, of course, one can shoot.'

'You shoot?' asked Herrick.

'Yes, I am what you would call a fine shot,' said Attwater. 'It is faith; I believe my balls will go true; if I were to miss once, it would spoil me for nine months.'

'You never miss, then?' said Herrick.

'Not unless I mean to,' said Attwater. 'But to miss nicely is the art. There was an old king one knew in the western islands, who used to empty a Winchester all round a man, and stir his hair or nick a rag out of his clothes with every ball except the last; and that went plump between the eyes. It was pretty practice.'

'You could do that?' asked Herrick, with a sudden chill.

'Oh, I can do anything,' returned the other. 'You do not understand: what must be, must.'

They were now come near to the back part of the house. One of the men was engaged about the cooking fire, which burned with the clear, fierce, essential radiance of cocoanut shells. A fragrance of strange meats was in the air. All round in the verandahs lamps were lighted, so that the place shone abroad in the dusk of the trees with many complicated patterns of shadow.

'Come and wash your hands,' said Attwater, and led the way into a clean, matted room with a cot bed, a safe, or shelf or two of books in a glazed case, and an iron washing-stand. Presently he cried in the native, and there appeared for a moment in the doorway a plump and pretty young woman with a clean towel.

'Hullo!' cried Herrick, who now saw for the first time the fourth survivor of the pestilence, and was startled by the recollection of the captain's orders.

'Yes,' said Attwater, 'the whole colony lives about the house, what's left of it. We are all afraid of devils, if you please! and Taniera and she sleep in the front parlour, and the other boy on the verandah.'

'She is pretty,' said Herrick.

'Too pretty,' said Attwater. 'That was why I had her married. A man never knows when he may be inclined to be a fool about women; so when we were left alone, I had the pair of them to the chapel and performed the ceremony. She made a lot of fuss. I do not take at all the romantic view of marriage,' he explained.

'And that strikes you as a safeguard?' asked Herrick with amazement.

'Certainly. I am a plain man and very literal. *Whom God hath joined together*, are the words, I fancy. So one married them, and respects the marriage,' said Attwater.

'Ah!' said Herrick.

'You see, I may look to make an excellent marriage when I go home,' began Attwater, confidentially. 'I am rich. This safe alone' – laying his hand upon it – 'will be a moderate fortune, when I have the time to place the pearls upon the market. Here are ten years' accumulation from a lagoon, where I have had as many as ten divers going all day long; and I went further than people usually do in these waters, for I rotted a lot of shell, and did splendidly. Would you like to see them?'

This confirmation of the captain's guess hit Herrick hard, and he contained himself with difficulty. 'No, thank you, I think not,' said he. 'I do not care for pearls. I am very indifferent to all these . . .'

'Gewgaws?' suggested Attwater. 'And yet I believe you ought to cast an eye on my collection, which is really unique, and which – oh! it is the case with all of us and everything about us! – hangs by a hair. Today it groweth up and flourisheth; tomorrow it is cut down and cast into the oven. Today it is here and together in this safe; tomorrow – tonight! – it may be scattered. Thou fool, this night thy soul shall be required of thee.'

'I do not understand you,' said Herrick.

'Not?' said Attwater.

'You seem to speak in riddles,' said Herrick, unsteadily. 'I do not understand what manner of man you are, nor what you are driving at.'

Attwater stood with his hands upon his hips, and his head bent forward. 'I am a fatalist,' he replied, 'and just now (if you insist on it) an experimentalist. Talking of which, by the bye, who painted out the schooner's name?' he said, with mocking softness, 'because, do you know? one thinks it should be done again. It can still be partly read; and whatever is worth doing, is surely worth doing well. You think with me? That is so nice! Well, shall we step on the verandah? I have a dry sherry that I would like your opinion of.'

Herrick followed him forth to where, under the light of the hanging lamps, the table shone with napery and crystal; followed him as the criminal goes with the hangman, or the sheep with the butcher; took the sherry mechanically, drank it, and spoke mechanical words of praise. The object of his terror had become suddenly inverted; till then he had seen Attwater trussed and gagged, a helpless victim, and had longed to run in and save him; he saw him now tower up mysterious and menacing, the angel of the Lord's wrath, armed with knowledge and threatening judgment. He set down his glass again, and was surprised to see it empty.

'You go always armed?' he said, and the next moment could have plucked his tongue out.

'Always,' said Attwater. 'I have been through a mutiny here; that was one of my incidents of missionary life.'

And just then the sound of voices reached them, and looking forth from the verandah they saw Huish and the captain drawing near.

Chapter 9
THE DINNER PARTY

They sat down to an island dinner, remarkable for its variety and excellence; turtle soup and steak, fish, fowls, a sucking pig, a cocoanut salad, and sprouting cocoanut roasted for dessert. Not a tin had been opened; and save for the oil and vinegar in the salad, and some green spears of onion which Attwater cultivated and plucked with his own hand, not even the condiments were European. Sherry, hock, and claret succeeded each other, and the *Farallone* champagne brought up the rear with the dessert.

It was plain that, like so many of the extremely religious in the days before teetotalism, Attwater had a dash of the epicure. For such characters it is softening to eat well; doubly so to have designed and had prepared an excellent meal for others; and the manners of their host were agreeably mollified in consequence. A cat of huge growth sat on his shoulders purring, and occasionally, with a deft paw, capturing a morsel in the air. To a cat he might be likened himself, as he lolled at the head of his table, dealing out attentions and innuendoes, and using the velvet and the claw indifferently. And both Huish and the captain fell progressively under the charm of his hospitable freedom.

Over the third guest, the incidents of the dinner may be said to have passed for long unheeded. Herrick accepted all that was offered him, ate and drank without tasting, and heard without comprehension. His mind was singly occupied in contemplating the horror of the circumstances in which he sat. What Attwater knew, what the captain designed, from which side treachery was to be first expected, these were the ground of his thoughts. There were times when he longed to throw down the table and flee into the night. And even that was debarred him; to do anything, to say anything, to move at all, were only to precipitate the barbarous tragedy; and he sat spellbound, eating with white

lips. Two of his companions observed him narrowly, Attwater
with raking, sidelong glances that did not interrupt his talk, the
captain with a heavy and anxious consideration.

'Well, I must say this sherry is a really prime article,' said
Huish. ''Ow much does it stand you in, if it's a fair question?'

'A hundred and twelve shillings in London, and the freight to
Valparaiso, and on again,' said Attwater. 'It strikes one as really
not a bad fluid.'

'A 'undred and twelve!' murmured the clerk, relishing the
wine and the figures in a common ecstasy: 'O my!'

'So glad you like it,' said Attwater. 'Help yourself, Mr Whish,
and keep the bottle by you.'

'My friend's name is Huish and not Whish, sir,' said the
captain with a flush.

'I beg your pardon, I am sure. Huish and not Whish,
certainly,' said Attwater. 'I was about to say that I have still
eight dozen,' he added, fixing the captain with his eye.

'Eight dozen what?' said Davis.

'Sherry,' was the reply. 'Eight dozen excellent sherry. Why, it
seems almost worth it in itself; to a man fond of wine.'

The ambiguous words struck home to guilty consciences, and
Huish and the captain sat up in their places and regarded him
with a scare.

'Worth what?' said Davis.

'A hundred and twelve shillings,' replied Attwater.

The captain breathed hard for a moment. He reached out far
and wide to find any coherency in these remarks; then, with a
great effort, changed the subject.

'I allow we are about the first white men upon this island, sir,'
said he.

Attwater followed him at once, and with entire gravity, to the
new ground. 'Myself and Dr Symonds excepted, I should say
the only ones,' he returned. 'And yet who can tell? In the course
of the ages someone may have lived here, and we sometimes
think that someone must. The cocoa palms grow all round the
island, which is scarce like nature's planting. We found besides,
when we landed, an unmistakable cairn upon the beach; use

unknown; but probably erected in the hope of gratifying some mumbo jumbo whose very name is forgotten, by some thick-witted gentry whose very bones are lost. Then the island (witness the *Directory*) has been twice reported; and since my tenancy, we have had two wrecks, both derelict. The rest is conjecture.'

'Dr Symonds is your partner, I guess?' said Davis.

'A dear fellow, Symonds! How he would regret it, if he knew you had been here!' said Attwater.

''E's on the *Trinity 'All*, ain't he?' asked Huish.

'And if you could tell me where the *Trinity 'All* was, you would confer a favour, Mr Whish!' was the reply.

'I suppose she has a native crew?' said Davis.

'Since the secret has been kept ten years, one would suppose she had,' replied Attwater.

'Well, now, see 'ere!' said Huish. 'You have everything about you in no end style, and no mistake, but I tell you it wouldn't do for me. Too much of "the old rustic bridge by the mill"; too retired, by 'alf. Give me the sound of Bow Bells!'

'You must not think it was always so,' replied Attwater. 'This was once a busy shore, although now, hark! you can hear the solitude. I find it stimulating. And talking of the sound of bells, kindly follow a little experiment of mine in silence.' There was a silver bell at his right hand to call the servants; he made them a sign to stand still, struck the bell with force, and leaned eagerly forward. The note rose clear and strong; it rang out clear and far into the night and over the deserted island; it died into the distance until there only lingered in the porches of the ear a vibration that was sound no longer. 'Empty houses, empty sea, solitary beaches!' said Attwater. 'And yet God hears the bell! And yet we sit in this verandah on a lighted stage with all heaven for spectators! And you call that solitude?'

There followed a bar of silence, during which the captain sat mesmerised.

Then Attwater laughed softly. 'These are the diversions of a lonely man,' he resumed, 'and possibly not in good taste. One tells oneself these little fairy tales for company. If there *should* happen to be anything in folk-lore, Mr Hay? But here comes the claret. One does not offer you Lafitte, captain, because I believe it is all sold to the railroad dining cars in your great country; but this Brâne-Mouton is of a good year, and Mr Whish will give me news of it.'

'That's a queer idea of yours!' cried the captain, bursting with a sigh from the spell that had bound him. 'So you mean to tell me now, that you sit here evenings and ring up . . . well, ring on the angels . . . by yourself?'

'As a matter of historic fact, and since you put it directly, one does not,' said Attwater. 'Why ring a bell, when there flows out from oneself and everything about one a far more momentous silence? the least beat of my heart and the least thought in my mind echoing into eternity for ever and for ever and for ever.'

'O look 'ere,' said Huish, 'turn down the lights at once, and the Band of 'Ope will oblige! This ain't a spiritual séance.'

'No folk-lore about Mr Whish – I beg your pardon, captain: Huish not Whish, of course,' said Attwater.

As the boy was filling Huish's glass, the bottle escaped from his hand and was shattered, and the wine spilt on the verandah floor. Instant grimness as of death appeared on the face of Attwater; he smote the bell imperiously, and the two brown natives fell into the attitude of attention and stood mute and trembling. There was just a moment of silence and hard looks; then followed a few savage words in the native; and, upon a gesture of dismissal, the service proceeded as before.

None of the party had as yet observed upon the excellent bearing of the two men. They were dark, undersized, and well set up; stepped softly, waited deftly, brought on the wines and dishes at a look, and their eyes attended studiously on their master.

'Where do you get your labour from anyway?' asked Davis.

'Ah, where not?' answered Attwater.

'Not much of a soft job, I suppose?' said the captain.

'If you will tell me where getting labour is!' said Attwater with a shrug. 'And of course, in our case, as we could name no destination, we had to go far and wide and do the best we could. We have gone as far west as the Kingsmills* and as far south as

Rapa-iti. Pity Symonds isn't here! He is full of yarns. That was his part, to collect them. Then began mine, which was the educational.'

'You mean to run them?' said Davis.

'Ay! to run them,' said Attwater.

'Wait a bit,' said Davis, 'I'm out of my depth. How was this? Do you mean to say you did it single-handed?'

'One did it single-handed,' said Attwater, 'because there was nobody to help one.'

'By God, but you must be a holy terror!' cried the captain, in a glow of admiration.

'One does one's best,' said Attwater.

'Well, now!' said Davis, 'I have seen a lot of driving in my time and been counted a good driver myself; I fought my way, third mate, round the Cape Horn with a push of packet rats that would have turned the devil out of hell and shut the door on him; and I tell you, this racket of Mr Attwater's takes the cake. In a ship, why, there ain't nothing to it! You've got the law with you, that's what does it. But put me down on this blame' beach alone, with nothing but a whip and a mouthful of bad words, and ask me to . . . no, *sir*! it's not good enough! I haven't got the sand for that!' cried Davis. 'It's the law behind,' he added; 'it's the law does it, every time!'

'The beak ain't as black as he's sometimes pynted,' observed Huish, humorously.

'Well, one got the law after a fashion,' said Attwater. 'One had to be a number of things. It was sometimes rather a bore.'

'I should smile!' said Davis. 'Rather lively, I should think!'

'I dare say we mean the same thing,' said Attwater. 'However, one way or another, one got it knocked into their heads that they *must* work, and they *did* . . . until the Lord took them!'

''Ope you made 'em jump,' said Huish.

'When it was necessary, Mr Whish, I made them jump,' said Attwater.

'You bet you did,' cried the captain. He was a good deal flushed, but not so much with wine as admiration; and his eyes drank in the huge proportions of the other with delight. 'You bet you did, and you bet that I can see you doing it! By God, you're a man, and you can say I said so.'

'Too good of you, I'm sure,' said Attwater.

'Did you – did you ever have crime here?' asked Herrick, breaking his silence with a pungent voice.

'Yes,' said Attwater, 'we did.'

'And how did you handle that, sir?' cried the eager captain.

'Well, you see, it was a queer case,' replied Attwater. 'It was a case that would have puzzled Solomon. Shall I tell it you? yes?'

The captain rapturously accepted.

'Well,' drawled Attwater, 'here is what it was. I dare say you know two types of natives, which may be called the obsequious and the sullen? Well, one had them, the types themselves, detected in the fact; and one had them together. Obsequiousness ran out of the first like wine out of a bottle, sullenness congested in the second. Obsequiousness was all smiles; he ran to catch your eye, he loved to gabble; and he had about a dozen words of beach English, and an eighth-of-an-inch veneer of Christianity. Sullens was industrious; a big down-looking bee. When he was spoken to, he answered with a black look and a shrug of one shoulder, but the thing would be done. I don't give him to you for a model of manners; there was nothing showy about Sullens; but he was strong and steady, and ungraciously obedient. Now Sullens got into trouble; no matter how; the regulations of the place were broken, and he was punished accordingly – without effect. So, the next day, and the next, and the day after, till I began to be weary of the business, and Sullens (I am afraid) particularly so. There came a day when he was in fault again, for the – oh, perhaps the thirtieth time; and he rolled a dull eye upon me, with a spark in it, and appeared to speak. Now the regulations of the place are formal upon one point: we allow no explanations; none are received, none allowed to be offered. So one stopped him instantly; but made a note of the circumstance. The next day, he was gone from the settlement. There could be nothing more annoying; if the labour took to running away, the fishery was wrecked. There are sixty miles of this island, you see, all in length like the Queen's Highway; the idea of pursuit in such a place was a piece of single-minded childishness, which one did not entertain. Two days later, I made a discovery; it came in upon me with a flash that Sullens had been unjustly punished from beginning to end, and the real culprit throughout had been Obsequiousness. The native who talks, like the woman who hesitates, is lost. You set him talking and lying; and he talks, and lies, and watches your face to see if he has pleased you; till at last, out comes the truth! It came out of Obsequiousness in the regular course. I said nothing to him; I dismissed him; and late as it was, for it was already night, set off to look for Sullens. I had not far to go: about two hundred yards up the island, the moon showed him to me. He was hanging in a cocoa palm – I'm not botanist enough to tell you how – but it's the way, in nine cases out of ten, these natives commit suicide. His tongue was out, poor devil, and the birds had got at him; I spare you details, he was an ugly sight! I gave the business six good hours of thinking in this verandah. My justice had been made a fool of; I don't suppose that I was ever angrier. Next day, I had the conch sounded and all hands out before sunrise. One took one's gun, and led the way, with Obsequiousness. He was very talkative; the beggar supposed that all was right now he had confessed; in the old schoolboy phrase, he was plainly 'sucking up' to me; full of protestations of goodwill and good behaviour; to which one answered one really can't remember what. Presently the tree came in sight, and the hanged man. They all burst out lamenting for their comrade in the island way, and Obsequiousness was the loudest of the mourners. He was quite genuine; a noxious creature, without any consciousness of guilt. Well, presently – to make a long story short – one told him to go up the tree. He stared a bit, looked at one with a trouble in his eye, and had rather a sickly smile; but went. He was obedient to the last; he had all the pretty virtues, but the truth was not in him. So soon as he was up, he looked down, and there was the rifle covering him; and at that he gave a whimper like a dog. You could hear a pin drop; no more keening now. There they all crouched upon the ground, with bulging eyes; there was he in the tree top, the colour of the lead; and between was the dead man, dancing a bit in the air. He was obedient to the last, recited his crime, recommended his soul to God. And then . . .'

Attwater paused, and Herrick, who had been listening attentively, made a convulsive movement which upset his glass.

'And then?' said the breathless captain.

'Shot,' said Attwater. 'They came to ground together.'

Herrick sprang to his feet with a shriek and an insensate gesture.

'It was a murder,' he screamed. 'A cold-hearted, bloody-minded murder! You monstrous being! Murderer and hypocrite – murderer and hypocrite – murderer and hypocrite—' he repeated, and his tongue stumbled among the words.

The captain was by him in a moment. 'Herrick!' he cried, 'behave yourself! Here, don't be a blame' fool!'

Herrick struggled in his embrace like a frantic child, and suddenly bowing his face in his hands, choked into a sob, the first of many, which now convulsed his body silently, and now jerked from him indescribable and meaningless sounds.

'Your friend appears over-excited,' remarked Attwater, sitting unmoved but all alert at table.

'It must be the wine,' replied the captain. 'He ain't no drinking man, you see. I – I think I'll take him away. A walk'll sober him up, I guess.'

He led him without resistance out of the verandah and into the night, in which they soon melted; but still for some time, as they drew away, his comfortable voice was to be heard soothing and remonstrating, and Herrick answering, at intervals, with the mechanical noises of hysteria.

''E's like a bloomin' poultry yard!' observed Huish, helping himself to wine (of which he spilled a good deal) with gentlemanly ease. 'A man should learn to beyave at table,' he added.

'Rather bad form, is it not?' said Attwater. 'Well, well, we are left *tête-à-tête*. A glass of wine with you, Mr Whish!'

Chapter 10
THE OPEN DOOR

The captain and Herrick meanwhile turned their back upon the lights in Attwater's verandah, and took a direction towards the pier and the beach of the lagoon.

The isle, at this hour, with its smooth floor of sand, the pillared roof overhead, and the prevalent illumination of the lamps, wore an air of unreality like a deserted theatre or a public garden at midnight. A man looked about him for the statues and tables. Not the least air of wind was stirring among the palms, and the silence was emphasised by the continuous clamour of the surf from the seashore, as it might be of traffic in the next street.

Still talking, still soothing him, the captain hurried his patient on, brought him at last to the lagoon side, and leading him down the beach, laved his head and face with the tepid water. The paroxysm gradually subsided, the sobs became less convulsive and then ceased; by an odd but not quite unnatural conjunction, the captain's soothing current of talk died away at the same time and by proportional steps, and the pair remained sunk in silence. The lagoon broke at their feet in petty wavelets, and with a sound as delicate as a whisper; stars of all degrees looked down on their own images in that vast mirror; and the more angry colour of the *Farallone's* riding lamp burned in the middle distance. For long they continued to gaze on the scene before them, and hearken anxiously to the rustle and tinkle of that miniature surf, or the more distant and loud reverberations from the outer coast. For long speech was denied them; and when the words came at last, they came to both simultaneously.

'Say, Herrick . . .' the captain was beginning.

But Herrick, turning swiftly towards his companion, bent him down with the eager cry: 'Let's up anchor, captain, and to sea!'

'Where to, my son?' said the captain. 'Up anchor's easy saying. But where to?'

'To sea,' responded Herrick. 'The sea's big enough! To sea – away from this dreadful island and that, oh! that sinister man!'

'Oh, we'll see about that,' said Davis. 'You brace up, and we'll see about that. You're all run down, that's what's wrong with you; you're all nerves, like Jemimar; you've got to brace up good and be yourself again, and then we'll talk.'

'To sea,' reiterated Herrick, 'to sea tonight – now – this moment!'

'It can't be, my son,' replied the captain firmly. 'No ship of mine puts to sea without provisions, you can take that for settled.'

'You don't seem to understand,' said Herrick. 'The whole thing is over, I tell you. There is nothing to do here, when he knows all. That man there with the cat knows all; can't you take it in?'

'All what?' asked the captain, visibly discomposed. 'Why, he received us like a perfect gentleman and treated us real handsome, until you began with your foolery – and I must say I seen men shot for less, and nobody sorry! What more do you expect anyway?'

Herrick rocked to and fro upon the sand, shaking his head.

'Guying us,' he said, 'he was guying us – only guying us; it's all we're good for.'

'There was one queer thing, to be sure,' admitted the captain, with a misgiving of the voice; 'that about the sherry. Damned if I caught on to that. Say, Herrick, you didn't give me away?'

'Oh! give you away!' repeated Herrick with weary, querulous scorn. 'What was there to give away? We're transparent; we've got rascal branded on us: detected rascal – detected rascal! Why, before he came on board, there was the name painted out, and he saw the whole thing. He made sure we would kill him there and then, and stood guying you and Huish on the chance. He calls that being frightened! Next he had me ashore; a fine time I had! *The two wolves,* he calls you and Huish. – *What is the puppy doing with the two wolves?* he asked. He showed me his pearls; he said they might be dispersed before morning, and *all hung by a hair* – and smiled as he said it, such a smile! O, it's no use, I tell you! He knows all, he sees through all; we only make him laugh with our pretences – he looks at us and laughs like God!'

There was a silence. Davis stood with contorted brows, gazing into the night.

'The pearls?' he said suddenly. 'He showed them to you? he has them?'

'No, he didn't show them; I forgot: only the safe they were in,' said Herrick. 'But you'll never get them!'

'I've two words to say to that,' said the captain.

'Do you think he would have been so easy at table, unless he was prepared?' cried Herrick. 'The servants were both armed. He was armed himself; he always is; he told me. You will never deceive his vigilance. Davis, I know it! It's all up; all up. There's nothing for it, there's nothing to be done: all gone: life, honour, love. Oh, my God, my God, why was I born?'

Another pause followed upon this outburst.

The captain put his hands to his brow.

'Another thing!' he broke out. 'Why did he tell you all this? Seems like madness to me!'

Herrick shook his head with gloomy iteration. 'You wouldn't understand if I were to tell you,' said he.

'I guess I can understand any blame' thing that you can tell me,' said the captain.

'Well, then, he's a fatalist,' said Herrick.

'What's that, a fatalist?' said Davis.

'Oh, it's a fellow that believes a lot of things,' said Herrick, 'believes that his bullets go true; believes that all falls out as God chooses, do as you like to prevent it; and all that.'

'Why, I guess I believe right so myself,' said Davis.

'You do?' said Herrick.

'You bet I do!' says Davis.

Herrick shrugged his shoulders. 'Well, you must be a fool,' said he, and he leaned his head upon his knees.

The captain stood biting his hands.

'There's one thing sure,' he said at last. 'I must get Huish out of that. *He's* not fit to hold his end up with a man like you describe.'

And he turned to go away. The words had been quite simple; not so the tone; and the other was quick to catch it.

'Davis!' he cried, 'no! Don't do it. Spare *me*, and don't do it – spare yourself, and leave it alone – for God's sake, for your children's sake!'

His voice rose to a passionate shrillness; another moment, and he might be overheard by their not distant victim. But Davis turned on him with a savage oath and gesture; and the miserable young man rolled over on his face on the sand, and lay speechless and helpless.

The captain meanwhile set out rapidly for Attwater's house. As he went, he considered with himself eagerly, his thoughts racing. The man had understood, he had mocked them from the beginning; he would teach him to make a mockery of John Davis! Herrick thought him a god; give him a second to aim in, and the god was overthrown. He chuckled as he felt the butt of his revolver. It should be done now, as he went in. From behind? It was difficult to get there. From across the table? No, the captain preferred to shoot standing, so as you could be sure to get your hand upon your gun. The best would be to summon Huish, and when Attwater stood up and turned – ah, then would be the moment. Wrapped in his ardent prefiguration of events, the captain posted towards the house with his head down.

'Hands up! Halt!' cried the voice of Attwater.

And the captain, before he knew what he was doing, had obeyed. The surprise was complete and irremediable. Coming on the top crest of his murderous intentions, he had walked straight into an ambuscade, and now stood, with his hands impotently lifted, staring at the verandah.

The party was now broken up. Attwater leaned on a post, and kept Davis covered with a Winchester. One of the servants was hard by with a second at the port arms, leaning a little forward, round-eyed with eager expectancy. In the open space

at the head of the stair, Huish was partly supported by the other
native; his face wreathed in meaningless smiles, his mind seem-
ingly sunk in the contemplation of an unlighted cigar.

'Well,' said Attwater, 'you seem to me to be a very twopenny
pirate!'

The captain uttered a sound in his throat for which we have
no name; rage choked him.

'I am going to give you Mr Whish – or the wine-sop that
remains of him,' continued Attwater. 'He talks a great deal
when he drinks, Captain Davis of the *Sea Ranger*. But I have
quite done with him – and return the article with thanks. Now,'
he cried sharply. 'Another false movement like that, and your
family will have to deplore the loss of an invaluable parent;
keep strictly still, Davis.'

Attwater said a word in the native, his eye still undeviatingly
fixed on the captain; and the servant thrust Huish smartly
forward from the brink of the stair. With an extraordinary
simultaneous dispersion of his members, that gentleman
bounded forth into space, struck the earth, ricocheted, and
brought up with his arms about a palm. His mind was quite a
stranger to these events; the expression of anguish that deformed
his countenance at the moment of the leap was probably
mechanical; and he suffered these convulsions in silence; clung
to the tree like an infant; and seemed, by his dips, to suppose
himself engaged in the pastime of bobbing for apples. A more
finely sympathetic mind or a more observant eye might have
remarked, a little in front of him on the sand, and still quite
beyond reach, the unlighted cigar.

'There is your Whitechapel carrion!' said Attwater. 'And now
you might very well ask me why I do not put a period to you
at once, as you deserve. I will tell you why, Davis. It is because I
have nothing to do with the *Sea Ranger* and the people you
drowned, or the *Farallone* and the champagne that you stole.
That is your account with God; He keeps it, and He will settle
it when the clock strikes. In my own case, I have nothing to go
on but suspicion, and I do not kill on suspicion, not even vermin
like you. But understand! if ever I see any of you again, it is

another matter, and you shall eat a bullet. And now take yourself off. March! and as you value what you call your life, keep your hands up as you go!'

The captain remained as he was, his hands up, his mouth open: mesmerised with fury.

'March!' said Attwater. 'One – two – three!'

And Davis turned and passed slowly away. But even as he went, he was meditating a prompt, offensive return. In the twinkling of an eye, he had leaped behind a tree; and was crouching there, pistol in hand, peering from either side of his place of ambush with bared teeth; a serpent already poised to strike. And already he was too late. Attwater and his servants had disappeared; and only the lamps shone on the deserted table and the bright sand about the house, and threw into the night in all directions the strong and tall shadows of the palms.

Davis ground his teeth. Where were they gone, the cowards? to what hole had they retreated beyond reach? It was in vain he should try anything, he, single and with a second-hand revolver, against three persons, armed with Winchesters, and who did not show an ear out of any of the apertures of that lighted and silent house? Some of them might have already ducked below it from the rear, and be drawing a bead upon him at that moment from the low-browed crypt, the receptacle of empty bottles and broken crockery. No, there was nothing to be done but to bring away (if it were still possible) his shattered and demoralised forces.

'Huish,' he said, 'come along.'

''S lose my ciga',' said Huish, reaching vaguely forward.

The captain let out a rasping oath. 'Come right along here,' said he.

''S all righ'. Sleep here 'th Atty-Attwa. Go boar' t'morr',' replied the festive one.

'If you don't come, and come now, by the living God, I'll shoot you!' cried the captain.

It is not to be supposed that the sense of these words in any way penetrated to the mind of Huish; rather that, in a fresh attempt upon the cigar, he overbalanced himself and came flying erratically forward: a course which brought him within reach of Davis.

'Now you walk straight,' said the captain, clutching him, 'or I'll know why not!'

"S lose my ciga',' replied Huish.

The captain's contained fury blazed up for a moment. He twisted Huish round, grasped him by the neck of the coat, ran him in front of him to the pier end, and flung him savagely forward on his face.

'Look for your cigar then, you swine!' said he, and blew his boat call till the pea in it ceased to rattle.

An immediate activity responded on board the *Farallone*; far away voices, and soon the sound of oars, floated along the surface of the lagoon; and at the same time, from nearer hand, Herrick aroused himself and strolled languidly up. He bent over the insignificant figure of Huish, where it grovelled, apparently insensible, at the base of the figure-head.

'Dead?' he asked.

'No, he's not dead,' said Davis.

'And Attwater?' asked Herrick.

'Now you just shut your head!' replied Davis. 'You can do that, I fancy, and by God, I'll show you how! I'll stand no more of your drivel.'

They waited accordingly in silence till the boat bumped on the furthest piers; then raised Huish, head and heels, carried him down the gangway, and flung him summarily in the bottom. On the way out he was heard murmuring of the loss of his cigar; and after he had been handed up the side like baggage, and cast down in the alleyway to slumber, his last audible expression was: 'Splen'l fl' Attwa'!' This the expert construed into 'Splendid fellow, Attwater'; with so much innocence had this great spirit issued from the adventures of the evening.

The captain went and walked in the waist with brief, irate turns; Herrick leaned his arms on the taffrail; the crew had all turned in. The ship had a gentle, cradling motion; at times a block piped like a bird. On shore, through the colonnade of palm stems, Attwater's house was to be seen shining steadily with many lamps. And there was nothing else visible, whether in the heaven above or in the lagoon below, but the stars and their reflections. It might have been minutes or it might have been hours, that Herrick leaned there, looking in the glorified water and drinking peace. 'A bath of stars,' he was thinking; when a hand was laid at last on his shoulder.

'Herrick,' said the captain, 'I've been walking off my trouble.'

A sharp jar passed through the young man, but he neither answered nor so much as turned his head.

'I guess I spoke a little rough to you on shore,' pursued the captain; 'the fact is, I was real mad; but now it's over, and you and me have to turn to and think.'

'I will *not* think,' said Herrick.

'Here, old man!' said Davis, kindly; 'this won't fight, you know! You've got to brace up and help me get things straight. You're not going back on a friend? That's not like you, Herrick!'

'O yes, it is,' said Herrick.

'Come, come!' said the captain, and paused as if quite at a loss. 'Look here,' he cried, 'you have a glass of champagne. *I* won't touch it, so that'll show you if I'm in earnest. But it's just the pick-me-up for you; it'll put an edge on you at once.'

'O, you leave me alone!' said Herrick, and turned away.

The captain caught him by the sleeve; and he shook him off and turned on him, for the moment, like a demoniac.

'Go to hell in your own way!' he cried.

And he turned away again, this time unchecked, and stepped forward to where the boat rocked alongside and ground occasionally against the schooner. He looked about him. A corner of the house was interposed between the captain and himself; all was well; no eye must see him in that last act. He slid silently into the boat; thence, silently, into the starry water. Instinctively he swam a little; it would be time enough to stop by and by.

The shock of the immersion brightened his mind immediately. The events of the ignoble day passed before him in a frieze of pictures, and he thanked 'whatever Gods there be' for that open door of suicide. In such a little while he would be done with it, the random business at an end, the prodigal son come home. A very bright planet shone before him and drew a trenchant wake along the water. He took that for his line and followed it. That was the last earthly thing that he should look upon; that radiant speck, which he had soon magnified into a City of Laputa,* along whose terraces there walked men and women of awful and benignant features, who viewed him with distant commiseration. These imaginary spectators consoled him; he told himself their talk, one to another; it was of himself and his sad destiny.

From such flights of fancy, he was aroused by the growing coldness of the water. Why should he delay? Here, where he was now, let him drop the curtain, let him seek the ineffable refuge, let him lie down with all races and generations of men in the house of sleep. It was easy to say, easy to do. To stop swimming: there was no mystery in that, if he could do it. Could he? And he could not. He knew it instantly. He was aware instantly of an opposition in his members, unanimous and invincible, clinging to life with a single and fixed resolve, finger by finger, sinew by sinew; something that was at once he and not he – at once within and without him; the shutting of some miniature valve in his brain, which a single manly thought should suffice to open – and the grasp of an external fate ineluctable as gravity. To any man there may come at times a consciousness that there blows, through all the articulations of his body, the wind of a spirit not wholly his; that his mind rebels; that another girds him and carries him whither he would not. It came now to Herrick, with the authority of a revelation. There was no escape possible. The open door was closed in his recreant face. He must go back into the world and amongst men without illusion. He must stagger on to the end with the pack of his responsibility and his disgrace, until a cold, a blow, a merciful chance ball, or the more merciful hangman, should dismiss him from his infamy. There were men who could commit suicide; there were men who could not; and he was one who could not.

For perhaps a minute, there raged in his mind the coil of this discovery; then cheerless certitude followed; and, with an incredible simplicity of submission to ascertained fact, he turned round and struck out for shore. There was a courage in this which he could not appreciate; the ignobility of his cowardice wholly occupying him. A strong current set against him like a wind in his face; he contended with it heavily, wearily, without enthusiasm, but with substantial advantage; marking his progress the while, without pleasure, by the outline of the trees. Once he had a moment of hope. He heard to the southward of him, towards the centre of the lagoon, the wallowing of some great fish, doubtless a shark, and paused for a little, treading water. Might not this be the hangman? he thought. But the wallowing died away; mere silence succeeded; and Herrick pushed on again for the shore, raging as he went at his own nature. Ay, he would wait for the shark; but if he had heard him coming! . . . His smile was tragic. He could have spat upon himself.

About three in the morning, chance, and the set of the current, and the bias of his own right-handed body, so decided it between them that he came to shore upon the beach in front of Attwater's. There he sat down, and looked forth into a world without any of the lights of hope. The poor diving dress of self-conceit was sadly tattered! With the fairy tale of suicide, of a refuge always open to him, he had hitherto beguiled and supported himself in the trials of life; and behold! that also was only a fairy tale, that also was folk-lore. With the consequences of his acts he saw himself implacably confronted for the duration of life: stretched upon a cross, and nailed there with the iron bolts of his own cowardice. He had no tears; he told himself no stories. His disgust with himself was so complete that even the process of apologetic mythology had ceased. He was like a man cast down from a pillar, and every bone broken. He lay there, and admitted the facts, and did not attempt to rise.

Dawn began to break over the far side of the atoll, the sky brightened, the clouds became dyed with gorgeous colours, the shadows of the night lifted. And, suddenly, Herrick was aware that the lagoon and the trees wore again their daylight livery;

and he saw, on board the *Farallone*, Davis extinguishing the lantern, and smoke rising from the galley.

Davis, without doubt, remarked and recognised the figure on the beach; or perhaps hesitated to recognise it; for after he had gazed a long while from under his hand, he went into the house and fetched a glass. It was very powerful; Herrick had often used it. With an instinct of shame, he hid his face in his hands.

'And what brings you here, Mr Herrick-Hay, or Mr Hay-Herrick?' asked the voice of Attwater. 'Your back view from my present position is remarkably fine, and I would continue to present it. We can get on very nicely as we are, and if you were to turn round, do you know? I think it would be awkward.'

Herrick slowly rose to his feet; his heart throbbed hard, a hideous excitement shook him, but he was master of himself. Slowly he turned, and faced Attwater and the muzzle of a pointed rifle. 'Why could I not do that last night?' he thought.

'Well, why don't you fire?' he said aloud, with a voice that trembled.

Attwater slowly put his gun under his arm, then his hands in his pockets.

'What brings you here?' he repeated.

'I don't know,' said Herrick; and then, with a cry: 'Can you do anything with me?'

'Are you armed?' said Attwater. 'I ask for the form's sake.'

'Armed? No!' said Herrick. 'O yes, I am, too!' And he flung upon the beach a dripping pistol.

'You are wet,' said Attwater.

'Yes, I am wet,' said Herrick. 'Can you do anything with me?'

Attwater read his face attentively.

'It would depend a good deal upon what you are,' said he.

'What I am? A coward!' said Herrick.

'There is very little to be done with that,' said Attwater. 'And yet the description hardly strikes one as exhaustive.'

'Oh, what does it matter?' cried Herrick. 'Here I am. I am broken crockery; I am a burst drum; the whole of my life is gone to water; I have nothing left that I believe in, except my living horror of myself. Why do I come to you? I don't know;

you are cold, cruel, hateful; and I hate you, or I think I hate you. But you are an honest man, an honest gentleman. I put myself, helpless, in your hands. What must I do? If I can't do anything, be merciful and put a bullet through me; it's only a puppy with a broken leg!'

'If I were you, I would pick up that pistol, come up to the house, and put on some dry clothes,' said Attwater.

'If you really mean it?' said Herrick. 'You know they – we – they . . . But you know all.'

'I know quite enough,' said Attwater. 'Come up to the house.'

And the captain, from the deck of the *Farallone*, saw the two men pass together under the shadow of the grove.

Chapter 11

DAVID AND GOLIATH

Huish had bundled himself up from the glare of the day – his face to the house, his knees retracted. The frail bones in the thin tropical raiment seemed scarce more considerable than a fowl's; and Davis, sitting on the rail with his arm about a stay, contemplated him with gloom, wondering what manner of counsel that insignificant figure should contain. For since Herrick had thrown him off and deserted to the enemy, Huish, alone of mankind, remained to him to be a helper and oracle.

He considered their position with a sinking heart. The ship was a stolen ship; the stores, either from initial carelessness or ill administration during the voyage, were insufficient to carry them to any port except back to Papeete; and there retribution waited in the shape of a gendarme, a judge with a queer-shaped hat, and the horror of distant Noumea.* Upon that side, there was no glimmer of hope. Here, at the island, the dragon was roused; Attwater with his men and his Winchesters watched and patrolled the house; let him who dare approach it. What else was then left but to sit there, inactive, pacing the decks – until the *Trinity Hall* arrived and they were cast into irons, or until the food came to an end, and the pangs of famine succeeded? For the *Trinity Hall* Davis was prepared; he would barricade the house, and die there defending it, like a rat in a crevice. But for the other? The cruise of the *Farallone*, into which he had plunged only a fortnight before, with such golden expectations, could this be the nightmare end of it? The ship rotting at anchor, the crew stumbling and dying in the scuppers? It seemed as if any extreme of hazard were to be preferred to so grisly a certainty; as if it would be better to up-anchor after all, put to sea at a venture, and, perhaps, perish at the hands of cannibals on one of the more obscure Paumotus. His eye roved swiftly over sea and sky in quest of any promise of wind, but the fountains of the Trade were empty. Where it had run yesterday and for weeks before, a roaring blue river charioting clouds, silence now reigned; and the whole height of the atmosphere stood balanced. On the endless ribbon of island that stretched out to either hand of him its array of golden and green and silvery palms, not the most volatile frond was to be seen stirring; they drooped to their stable images in the lagoon like things carved of metal, and already their long line began to reverberate heat. There was no escape possible that day, none probable on the morrow. And still the stores were running out!

Then came over Davis, from deep down in the roots of his being, or at least from far back among his memories of childhood and innocence, a wave of superstition. This run of ill luck was something beyond natural; the chances of the game were in themselves more various; it seemed as if the devil must serve the pieces. The devil? He heard again the clear note of Attwater's bell ringing abroad into the night, and dying away. How if God . . .?

Briskly, he averted his mind. Attwater: that was the point. Attwater had food and a treasure of pearls; escape made possible in the present, riches in the future. They must come to grips with Attwater; the man must die. A smoky heat went over his face, as he recalled the impotent figure he had made last night and the contemptuous speeches he must bear in silence. Rage, shame, and the love of life, all pointed the one way; and only invention halted: how to reach him? had he strength enough? was there any help in that misbegotten packet of bones against the house?

His eyes dwelled upon him with a strange avidity, as though he would read into his soul; and presently the sleeper moved, stirred uneasily, turned suddenly round, and threw him a blinking look. Davis maintained the same dark stare, and Huish looked away again and sat up.

'Lord, I've an 'eadache on me!' said he. 'I believe I was a bit swipey last night. W'ere's that cry-byby 'Errick?'

'Gone,' said the captain.

'Ashore?' cried Huish. 'Oh, I say! I'd 'a gone too.'

'Would you?' said the captain.

'Yes, I would,' replied Huish. 'I like Attwater. 'E's all right; we got on like one o'clock when you were gone. And ain't his sherry in it, rather? It's like Spiers and Ponds' Amontillado! I wish I 'ad a drain of it now.' He sighed.

'Well, you'll never get no more of it – that's one thing,' said Davis, gravely.

''Ere! wot's wrong with you, Dyvis? Coppers 'ot? Well, look at *me*! *I* ain't grumpy,' said Huish; 'I'm as plyful as a canary-bird, I am.'

'Yes,' said Davis, 'you're playful; I own that; and you were playful last night, I believe, and a damned fine performance you made of it.'

''Allo!' said Huish. ''Ow's this? Wot performance?'

'Well, I'll tell you,' said the captain, getting slowly off the rail.

And he did: at full length, with every wounding epithet and absurd detail repeated and emphasised; he had his own vanity and Huish's upon the grill, and roasted them; and as he spoke, he inflicted and endured agonies of humiliation. It was a plain man's masterpiece of the sardonic.

'What do you think of it?' said he, when he had done, and looked down at Huish, flushed and serious, and yet jeering.

'I'll tell you wot it is,' was the reply, 'you and me cut a pretty dicky figure.'

'That's so,' said Davis, 'a pretty measly figure, by God! And, by God, I want to see that man at my knees.'

'Ah!' said Huish. ''Ow to get him there?'

'That's it!' cried Davis. 'How to get hold of him! They're four to two; though there's only one man among them to count, and that's Attwater. Get a bead on Attwater, and the others would cut and run and sing out like frightened poultry – and old man Herrick would come round with his hat for a share of the pearls. No, *Sir*! it's how to get hold of Attwater! And we daren't even go ashore; he would shoot us in the boat like dogs.'

'Are you particular about having him dead or alive?' asked Huish.

'I want to see him dead,' said the captain.

'Ah, well!' said Huish, 'then I believe I'll do a bit of breakfast.' And he turned into the house.

The captain doggedly followed him.

'What's this?' he asked. 'What's your idea, anyway?'

'Oh, you let me alone, will you?' said Huish, opening a bottle of champagne. 'You'll 'ear my idea soon enough. Wyte till I pour some cham on my 'ot coppers.' He drank a glass off, and affected to listen. ''Ark!' said he, ''ear it fizz. Like 'am fryin', I declyre. 'Ave a glass, do, and look sociable.'

'No!' said the captain, with emphasis; 'no, I will not! there's business.'

'You p'ys your money and you tykes your choice, my little man,' returned Huish. 'Seems rather a shyme to me to spoil your breakfast for wot's really ancient 'istory.'

He finished three parts of a bottle of champagne, and nibbled a corner of biscuit, with extreme deliberation; the captain sitting opposite and champing the bit like an impatient horse. Then Huish leaned his arms on the table and looked Davis in the face.

'W'en you're ready!' said he.

'Well, now, what's your idea?' said Davis, with a sigh.

'Fair play!' said Huish. 'What's yours?'

'The trouble is that I've got none,' replied Davis; and wandered for some time in aimless discussion of the difficulties in their path, and useless explanations of his own fiasco.

'About done?' said Huish.

'I'll dry up right here,' replied Davis.

'Well, then,' said Huish, 'you give me your 'and across the table, and say, "Gawd strike me dead if I don't back you up."'

His voice was hardly raised, yet it thrilled the hearer. His face seemed the epitome of cunning, and the captain recoiled from it as from a blow.

'What for?' said he.

'Luck,' said Huish. 'Substantial guarantee demanded.'

And he continued to hold out his hand.

'I don't see the good of any such tomfoolery,' said the other.

'I do, though,' returned Huish. 'Gimme your 'and and say the words; then you'll 'ear my view of it. Don't, and you won't.'

The captain went through the required form, breathing short, and gazing on the clerk with anguish. What to fear, he knew not; yet he feared slavishly what was to fall from the pale lips.

'Now, if you'll excuse me 'alf a second,' said Huish, 'I'll go and fetch the byby.'

'The baby?' said Davis. 'What's that?'

'Fragile. With care. This side up,' replied the clerk with a wink, as he disappeared.

He returned, smiling to himself, and carrying in his hand a silk handkerchief. The long stupid wrinkles ran up Davis's brow, as he saw it. What should it contain? He could think of nothing more recondite than a revolver.

Huish resumed his seat.

'Now,' said he, 'are you man enough to take charge of 'Errick and the niggers? Because I'll take care of Hattwater.'

'How?' cried Davis. 'You can't!'

'Tut, tut!' said the clerk. 'You gimme time. Wot's the first point? The first point is that we can't get ashore, and I'll make you a present of that for a 'ard one. But 'ow about a flag of truce? Would that do the trick, d'ye think? or would Attwater simply blyze aw'y at us in the bloomin' boat like dawgs?'

'No,' said Davis, 'I don't believe he would.'

'No more do I,' said Huish; 'I don't believe he would either; and I'm sure I 'ope he won't! So then you can call us ashore. Next point is to get near the managin' direction. And for that I'm going to 'ave you write a letter, in w'ich you s'y you're ashamed to meet his eye, and that the bearer, Mr J. L. 'Uish, is empowered to represent you. Armed with w'ich seemin'ly simple expedient, Mr J. L. 'Uish will proceed to business.'

He paused, like one who had finished, but still held Davis with his eye.

'How?' said Davis. 'Why?'

'Well, you see, you're big,' returned Huish; ''e knows you 'ave a gun in your pocket, and anybody can see with 'alf an eye that you ain't the man to 'esitate about usin' it. So it's no go with you, and never was; you're out of the runnin', Dyvis. But he won't be afryde of me, I'm such a little un! I'm unarmed – no kid about that – and I'll hold my 'ands up right enough.' He paused. 'If I can manage to sneak up nearer to him as we talk,' he resumed, 'you look out and back me up smart. If I don't, we go aw'y again, and nothink to 'urt. See?'

The captain's face was contorted by the frenzied effort to comprehend.

'No, I don't see,' he cried, 'I can't see. What do you mean?'

'I mean to do for the Beast!' cried Huish, in a burst of venomous triumph. 'I'll bring the 'ulkin' bully to grass. He's 'ad his larks out of me; I'm goin' to 'ave my lark out of 'im, and a good lark too!'

'What is it?' said the captain, almost in a whisper.

'Sure you want to know?' asked Huish.

Davis rose and took a turn in the house.

'Yes, I want to know,' he said at last with an effort.

'We'n you're back's at the wall, you do the best you can, don't you?' began the clerk. 'I s'y that, because I 'appen to know there's a prejudice against it; it's considered vulgar, awf'ly vulgar.' He unrolled the handkerchief and showed a four-ounce jar. 'This 'ere's vitriol, this is,' said he.

The captain stared upon him with a whitening face.

'This is the stuff!' he pursued, holding it up. 'This'll burn to the bone; you'll see it smoke upon 'im like 'ell fire! One drop upon 'is bloomin' heyesight, and I'll trouble you for Attwater!'

'No, no, by God!' exclaimed the captain.

'Now, see 'ere, ducky,' said Huish, 'this is my bean feast, I believe? I'm goin' up to that man single-'anded, I am. 'E's about seven foot high, and I'm five foot one. 'E's a rifle in his 'and, 'e's on the look-out, 'e wasn't born yesterday. This is Dyvid and Goliar, I tell you! If I'd ast you to walk up and face the music I could understand. But I don't. I on'y ast you to stand by and spifflicate the niggers. It'll all come in quite natural; you'll see, else! Fust thing, you know, you'll see him running round and 'owling like a good un . . .'

'Don't!' said Davis. 'Don't talk of it!'

'Well, you *are* a juggins!' exclaimed Huish. 'What did you want? You wanted to kill him, and tried to last night. You wanted to kill the 'ole lot of them and tried to, and 'ere I show you 'ow; and because there's some medicine in a bottle you kick up this fuss!'

'I suppose that's so,' said Davis. 'It don't seem someways reasonable, only there it is.'

'It's the happlication of science, I suppose?' sneered Huish.

'I don't know what it is,' cried Davis, pacing the floor; 'it's there! I draw the line at it. I can't put a finger to no such piggishness. It's too damned hateful!'

'And I suppose it's all your fancy pynted it,' said Huish, 'w'en you take a pistol and a bit o' lead, and copse a man's brains all over him? No accountin' for tystes.'

'I'm not denying it,' said Davis, 'it's something here, inside of me. It's foolishness; I dare say it's dam foolishness. I don't argue, I just draw the line. Isn't there no other way?'

'Look for yourself,' said Huish. 'I ain't wedded to this, if you think I am; I ain't ambitious; I don't make a point of playin' the lead; I offer to, that's all, and if you can't show me better, by Gawd, I'm goin' to!'

'Then the risk!' cried Davis.

'If you ast me straight, I should say it was a case of seven to one and no takers,' said Huish. 'But that's my look-out, ducky, and I'm gyme, that's wot I am: gyme all through.'

The captain looked at him. Huish sat there, preening his sinister vanity, glorying in his precedency in evil; and the villainous courage and readiness of the creature shone out of him like a candle from a lantern. Dismay and a kind of respect seized hold on Davis in his own despite. Until that moment, he had seen the clerk always hanging back, always listless, uninterested, and openly grumbling at a word of anything to do; and now, by the touch of an enchanter's wand, he beheld him sitting girt and resolved, and his face radiant. He had raised the devil, he thought; and asked who was to control him? and his spirits quailed.

'Look as long as you like,' Huish was going on. 'You don't

see any green in my eye! I ain't afryde of Attwater, I ain't afryde of you, and I ain't afryde of words. You want to kill people, that's wot *you* want; but you want to do it in kid gloves, and it can't be done that w'y. Murder ain't genteel, it ain't easy, it ain't safe, and it tykes a man to do it. 'Ere's the man.'

'Huish!' began the captain with energy; and then stopped, and remained staring at him with corrugated brows.

'Well, hout with it!' said Huish. ''Ave you anythink else to put up? Is there any other chanst to try?'

The captain held his peace.

'There you are then!' said Huish with a shrug.

Davis fell again to his pacing.

'Oh, you may do sentry-go till you're blue in the mug, you won't find anythink else,' said Huish.

There was a little silence; the captain, like a man launched on a swing, flying dizzily among extremes of conjecture and refusal.

'But see,' he said, suddenly pausing. 'Can you? Can the thing be done? It – it can't be easy.'

'If I get within twenty foot of 'im it'll be done; so you look out,' said Huish, and his tone of certainty was absolute.

'How can you know that?' broke from the captain in a choked cry. 'You beast, I believe you've done it before!'

'Oh, that's private affyres,' returned Huish, 'I ain't a talking man.'

A shock of repulsion struck and shook the captain; a scream rose almost to his lips; had he uttered it, he might have cast himself at the same moment on the body of Huish, might have picked him up, and flung him down, and wiped the cabin with him, in a frenzy of cruelty that seemed half moral. But the moment passed; and the abortive crisis left the man weaker. The stakes were so high – the pearls on the one hand – starvation and shame on the other. Ten years of pearls! The imagination of Davis translated them into a new, glorified existence for himself and his family. The seat of this new life must be in London; there were deadly reasons against Portland, Maine; and the pictures that came to him were of English manners. He saw his boys marching in the procession of a school, with gowns on, an usher marshalling them and reading as he walked in a great book. He was installed in a villa, semi-detached; the name, *Rosemore*, on the gateposts. In a chair on the gravel walk, he seemed to sit smoking a cigar, a blue ribbon in his buttonhole, victor over himself and circumstances, and the malignity of bankers. He saw the parlour with red curtains and shells on the mantelpiece – and with the fine inconsistency of visions, mixed a grog at the mahogany table ere he turned in. With that the *Farallone* gave one of the aimless and nameless movements which (even in an anchored ship and even in the most profound calm) remind one of the mobility of fluids; and he was back again under the cover of the house, the fierce daylight besieging it all round and glaring in the chinks, and the clerk in a rather airy attitude, awaiting his decision.

He began to walk again. He aspired after the realisation of these dreams, like a horse nickering for water; the lust of them burned in his inside. And the only obstacle was Attwater, who had insulted him from the first. He gave Herrick a full share of the pearls, he insisted on it; Huish opposed him, and he trod the opposition down; and praised himself exceedingly. He was not going to use vitriol himself; was he Huish's keeper? It was a pity he had asked, but after all! . . . he saw the boys again in the school procession, with the gowns he had thought to be so 'tony' long since . . . And at the same time the incomparable shame of the last evening blazed up in his mind.

'Have it your own way!' he said hoarsely.

'Oh, I knew you would walk up,' said Huish. 'Now for the letter. There's paper, pens and ink. Sit down and I'll dictyte.'

The captain took a seat and the pen, looked a while helplessly at the paper, then at Huish. The swing had gone the other way; there was a blur upon his eyes. 'It's a dreadful business,' he said, with a strong twitch of his shoulders.

'It's rather a start, no doubt,' said Huish. 'Tyke a dip of ink. That's it. *William John Hattwater, Esq., Sir*': he dictated

'How do you know his name is William John?' asked Davis.

'Saw it on a packing case,' said Huish. 'Got that?'

'No,' said Davis. 'But there's another thing. What are we to write?'

'O my golly!' cried the exasperated Huish. 'Wot kind of man do *you* call yourself? *I'm* goin' to tell you wot to write; that's *my* pitch; if you'll just be so bloomin' condescendin' as to write it down! *William John Attwater, Esq., Sir*': he reiterated. And the captain at last beginning half mechanically to move his pen, the dictation proceeded:

It is with feelings of shyme and 'artfelt contrition that I approach you after the yumiliatin' events of last night. Our Mr 'Errick has left the ship, and will have doubtless communicated to you the nature of our 'opes. Needless to s'y, these are no longer possible: Fate 'as declyred against us, and we bow the 'ead. Well awyre as I am of the just suspicions with w'ich I am regarded, I do not venture to solicit the fyvour of an interview for myself, but in order to put an end to a situytion w'ich must be equally pyneful to all, I 'ave deputed my friend and partner, Mr J. L. Huish, to l'y before you my proposals, and w'ich by their moderytion, will, I trust, be found to merit your attention. Mr J. L. Huish is entirely unarmed, I swear to Gawd! and will 'old 'is 'ands over 'is 'ead from the moment he begins to approach you. I am your fytheful servant, John Davis.

Huish read the letter with the innocent joy of amateurs, chuckled gustfully to himself, and reopened it more than once after it was folded, to repeat the pleasure; Davis meanwhile sitting inert and heavily frowning.

Of a sudden he rose; he seemed all abroad. 'No!' he cried. 'No! it can't be! It's too much; it's damnation. God would never forgive it.'

'Well, and 'oo wants Him to?' returned Huish, shrill with fury. 'You were damned years ago for the *Sea Rynger*, and said so yourself. Well then, be damned for something else, and 'old your tongue.'

The captain looked at him mistily. 'No,' he pleaded, 'no, old man! don't do it.'

''Ere now,' said Huish, 'I'll give you my ultimytum. Go or st'y w'ere you are; I don't mind; I'm goin' to see that man and chuck this vitriol in his eyes. If you st'y I'll go alone; the niggers will likely knock me on the 'ead, and a fat lot you'll be the better! But there's one thing sure: I'll 'ear no more of your moonin', mullygrubbin' rot, and tyke it stryte.'

The captain took it with a blink and a gulp. Memory, with phantom voices, repeated in his ears something similar, something he had once said to Herrick – years ago it seemed.

'Now, gimme over your pistol,' said Huish. 'I 'ave to see all clear. Six shots, and mind you don't wyste them.'

The captain, like a man in a nightmare, laid down his revolver on the table, and Huish wiped the cartridges and oiled the works.

It was close on noon, there was no breath of wind, and the heat was scarce bearable, when the two men came on deck, had the boat manned, and passed down, one after another, into the stern-sheets. A white shirt at the end of an oar served as a flag of truce; and the men, by direction, and to give it the better chance to be observed, pulled with extreme slowness. The isle shook before them like a place incandescent; on the face of the lagoon blinding copper suns, no bigger than sixpences, danced and stabbed them in the eyeballs; there went up from sand and sea, and even from the boat, a glare of scathing brightness; and as they could only peer abroad from between closed lashes, the excess of light seemed to be changed into a sinister darkness, comparable to that of a thundercloud before it bursts.

The captain had come upon this errand for any one of a dozen reasons, the last of which was desire for its success. Superstition rules all men; semi-ignorant and gross natures, like that of Davis, it rules utterly. For murder he had been prepared; but this horror of the medicine in the bottle went beyond him, and he seemed to himself to be parting the last strands that united him to God. The boat carried him on to reprobation, to damnation; and he suffered himself to be carried passively consenting, silently bidding farewell to his better self and his hopes.

Huish sat by his side in towering spirits that were not wholly genuine. Perhaps as brave a man as ever lived, brave as a weasel, he must still reassure himself with the tones of his own voice; he must play his part to exaggeration, he must out-Herod Herod, insult all that was respectable, and brave all that was formidable, in a kind of desperate wager with himself.

'Golly, but it's 'ot!' said he. 'Cruel 'ot, I call it. Nice d'y to get your gruel in! I s'y, you know, it must feel awf'ly peculiar to get bowled over on a d'y like this. I'd rather 'ave it on a cowld and frosty morning, wouldn't you? (Singing) "'*Ere we go round the mulberry bush on a cowld and frosty mornin'*." (Spoken) Give you my word, I 'aven't thought o' that in ten year; used to sing it at a hinfant school in 'Ackney, 'Ackney Wick it was. (Singing) "*This is the way the tyler does, the tyler does.*' (Spoken) Bloomin' 'umbug. 'Ow are you off now, for the notion of a future styte? Do you cotton to the tea-fight views, or the old red 'ot boguey business?'

'Oh, dry up!' said the captain.

'No, but I want to know,' said Huish. 'It's within the sp'ere of practical politics for you and me, my boy; we may both be bowled over, one up, t'other down, within the next ten minutes. It would be rather a lark, now, if you only skipped across, came up smilin' t'other side, and a hangel met you with a B. and S. under his wing. 'Ullo, you'd s'y: come, I tyke this kind.'

The captain groaned. While Huish was thus airing and exercising his bravado, the man at his side was actually engaged in prayer. Prayer, what for? God knows. But out of his inconsistent, illogical, and agitated spirit, a stream of supplication was poured forth, inarticulate as himself, earnest as death and judgment.

'Thou Gawd seest me!' continued Huish. 'I remember I had that written in my Bible. I remember the Bible too, all about Abinadab and parties. Well, Gawd!' apostrophising the meridian, 'you're goin' to see a rum start presently, I promise you that!'

The captain bounded.

'I'll have no blasphemy!' he cried, 'no blasphemy in my boat.'

'All right, cap,' said Huish. 'Anythink to oblige. Any other topic you would like to sudgest, the rynegyge, the lightnin' rod, Shykespeare, or the musical glasses?* 'Ere's conversation on a tap. Put a penny in the slot, and . . . 'ullo! 'ere they are!' he cried. 'Now or never is 'e goin' to shoot?'

And the little man straightened himself into an alert and dashing attitude, and looked steadily at the enemy.

But the captain rose half up in the boat with eyes protruding. 'What's that?' he cried.

'Wot's wot?' said Huish.

'Those – blamed things,' said the captain.

And indeed it was something strange. Herrick and Attwater, both armed with Winchesters, had appeared out of the grove behind the figure-head; and to either hand of them, the sun glistened upon two metallic objects, locomotory like men, and occupying in the economy of these creatures the places of heads – only the heads were faceless. To Davis between wind and water, his mythology appeared to have come alive, and Tophet* to be vomiting demons. But Huish was not mystified a moment.

'Divers' 'elmets, you ninny. Can't you see?' he said.

'So they are,' said Davis, with a gasp. 'And why? Oh, I see, it's for armour.'

'Wot did I tell you?' said Huish. 'Dyvid and Goliar all the w'y and back.'

The two natives (for they it was that were equipped in this unusual panoply of war) spread out to right and left, and at last lay down in the shade, on the extreme flank of the position. Even now that the mystery was explained, Davis was hatefully preoccupied, stared at the flame on their crests, and forgot, and then remembered with a smile, the explanation.

Attwater withdrew again into the grove, and Herrick, with his gun under his arm, came down the pier alone.

About half-way down he halted and hailed the boat.

'What do you want?' he cried.

'I'll tell that to Mr Attwater,' replied Huish, stepping briskly on the ladder. 'I don't tell it to you, because you played the trucklin' sneak. Here's a letter for him: tyke it, and give it, and be 'anged to you!'

'Davis, is this all right?' said Herrick.

Davis raised his chin, glanced swiftly at Herrick and away again, and held his peace. The glance was charged with some deep emotion, but whether of hatred or of fear, it was beyond Herrick to divine.

'Well,' he said, 'I'll give the letter.' He drew a score with his foot on the boards of the gangway. 'Till I bring the answer, don't move a step past this.'

And he returned to where Attwater leaned against a tree, and gave him the letter. Attwater glanced it through.

'What does that mean?' he asked, passing it to Herrick. 'Treachery?'

'Oh, I suppose so!' said Herrick.

'Well, tell him to come on,' said Attwater. 'One isn't a fatalist for nothing. Tell him to come on and to look out.'

Herrick returned to the figure-head. Half-way down the pier the clerk was waiting, with Davis by his side.

'You are to come along, Huish,' said Herrick. 'He bids you look out, no tricks.'

Huish walked briskly up the pier, and paused face to face with the young man.

'W'ere is 'e?' said he, and to Herrick's surprise, the low-bred, insignificant face before him flushed suddenly crimson and went white again.

'Right forward,' said Herrick, pointing. 'Now your hands above your head.'

The clerk turned away from him and towards the figure-head, as though he were about to address to it his devotions; he was seen to heave a deep breath; and raised his arms. In common with many men of his unhappy physical endowments, Huish's hands were disproportionately long and broad, and the palms in particular enormous; a four-ounce jar was nothing in that capacious fist. The next moment he was plodding steadily forward on his mission.

Herrick at first followed. Then a noise in his rear startled him, and he turned about to find Davis already advanced as far as the figure-head. He came, crouching and open-mouthed, as the

mesmerised may follow the mesmeriser; all human consider-
ations, and even the care of his own life, swallowed up in one
abominable and burning curiosity.

'Halt!' cried Herrick, covering him with his rifle. 'Davis, what
are you doing, man? *You* are not to come.'

Davis instinctively paused, and regarded him with a dreadful
vacancy of eye.

'Put your back to that figure-head, do you hear me? and stand
fast!' said Herrick.

The captain fetched a breath, stepped back against the figure-
head, and instantly redirected his glances after Huish.

There was a hollow place of the sand in that part, and, as it
were, a glade among the cocoa palms in which the direct
noonday sun blazed intolerably. At the far end, in the shadow,
the tall figure of Attwater was to be seen leaning on a tree;
towards him, with his hands over his head, and his steps
smothered in the sand, the clerk painfully waded. The surround-
ing glare threw out and exaggerated the man's smallness; it
seemed no less perilous an enterprise, this that he was gone
upon, than for a whelp to besiege a citadel.

'There, Mr Whish. That will do,' cried Attwater. 'From that
distance, and keeping your hands up, like a good boy, you can
very well put me in possession of the skipper's views.'

The interval betwixt them was perhaps forty feet; and Huish
measured it with his eye, and breathed a curse. He was already
distressed with labouring in the loose sand, and his arms ached
bitterly from their unnatural position. In the palm of his right
hand, the jar was ready; and his heart thrilled, and his voice
choked, as he began to speak.

'Mr Hattwater,' said he, 'I don't know if ever you 'ad a
mother . . .'

'I can set your mind at rest: I had,' returned Attwater; 'and
henceforth, if I might venture to suggest it, her name need not
recur in our communications. I should perhaps tell you that I
am not amenable to the pathetic.'

'I am sorry, sir, if I 'ave seemed to tresparse on your private
feelin's,' said the clerk, cringing and stealing a step. 'At least,

sir, you will never pe'suade me that you are not a perfec' gentleman; I know a gentleman when I see him; and as such, I 'ave no 'esitation in throwin' myself on your merciful consideration. It *is* 'ard lines, no doubt; it's 'ard lines to have to hown yourself beat; it's 'ard lines to 'ave to come and beg to you for charity.'

'When, if things had only gone right, the whole place was as good as your own?' suggested Attwater. 'I can understand the feeling.'

'You are judging me, Mr Attwater,' said the clerk, 'and God knows how unjustly! *Thou Gawd seest me*, was the tex' I 'ad in my Bible, w'ich my father wrote it in with 'is own 'and upon the fly leaft.'

'I am sorry I have to beg your pardon once more,' said Attwater; 'but, do you know, you seem to me to be a trifle nearer, which is entirely outside of our bargain. And I would venture to suggest that you take one – two – three – steps back; and stay there.'

The devil, at this staggering disappointment, looked out of Huish's face, and Attwater was swift to suspect. He frowned, he stared on the little man, and considered. Why should he be creeping nearer? The next moment, his gun was at his shoulder.

'Kindly oblige me by opening your hands. Open your hands wide – let me see the fingers spread, you dog – throw down that thing you're holding!' he roared, his rage and certitude increasing together.

And then, at almost the same moment, the indomitable Huish decided to throw, and Attwater pulled the trigger. There was scarce the difference of a second between the two resolves, but it was in favour of the man with the rifle; and the jar had not yet left the clerk's hand, before the ball shattered both. For the twinkling of an eye the wretch was in hell's agonies, bathed in liquid flames, a screaming bedlamite; and then a second and more merciful bullet stretched him dead.

The whole thing was come and gone in a breath. Before Herrick could turn about, before Davis could complete his cry of horror, the clerk lay in the sand, sprawling and convulsed.

Attwater ran to the body; he stooped and viewed it; he put his finger in the vitriol, and his face whitened and hardened with anger.

Davis had not yet moved; he stood astonished, with his back to the figure-head, his hands clutching it behind him, his body inclined forward from the waist.

Attwater turned deliberately and covered him with his rifle.

'Davis,' he cried, in a voice like a trumpet, 'I give you sixty seconds to make your peace with God!'

Davis looked, and his mind awoke. He did not dream of self-defence, he did not reach for his pistol. He drew himself up instead to face death, with a quivering nostril.

'I guess I'll not trouble the Old Man,' he said; 'considering the job I was on, I guess it's better business to just shut my face.'

Attwater fired; there came a spasmodic movement of the victim, and immediately above the middle of his forehead, a black hole marred the whiteness of the figure-head. A dreadful pause; then again the report, and the solid sound and jar of the bullet in the wood; and this time the captain had felt the wind of it along his cheek. A third shot, and he was bleeding from one ear; and along the levelled rifle Attwater smiled like a Red Indian.

The cruel game of which he was the puppet was now clear to Davis; three times he had drunk of death, and he must look to drink of it seven times more before he was despatched. He held up his hand.

'Steady!' he cried; 'I'll take your sixty seconds.'

'Good!' said Attwater.

The captain shut his eyes tight like a child: he held his hands up at last with a tragic and ridiculous gesture.

'My God, for Christ's sake, look after my two kids,' he said; and then, after a pause and a falter, 'for Christ's sake, Amen.'

And he opened his eyes and looked down the rifle with a quivering mouth.

'But don't keep fooling me long!' he pleaded.

'That's all your prayer?' asked Attwater, with a singular ring in his voice.

'Guess so,' said Davis.

'So?' said Attwater, resting the butt of his rifle on the ground, 'is that done? Is your peace made with Heaven? Because it is with me. Go, and sin no more, sinful father. And remember that whatever you do to others, God shall visit it again a thousand-fold upon your innocents.'

The wretched Davis came staggering forward from his place against the figure-head, fell upon his knees, and waved his hands, and fainted.

When he came to himself again, his head was on Attwater's arm, and close by stood one of the men in divers' helmets, holding a bucket of water, from which his late executioner now laved his face. The memory of that dreadful passage returned upon him in a clap; again he saw Huish lying dead, again he seemed to himself to totter on the brink of an unplumbed eternity. With trembling hands he seized hold of the man whom he had come to slay; and his voice broke from him like that of a child among the nightmares of fever: 'O! isn't there no mercy? O! what must I do to be saved?'

'Ah!' thought Attwater, 'here's the true penitent.'

Chapter 12
A TAIL-PIECE

On a very bright, hot, lusty, strongly blowing noon, a fortnight after the events recorded, and a month since the curtain rose upon this episode, a man might have been spied, praying on the sand by the lagoon beach. A point of palm trees isolated him from the settlement; and from the place where he knelt, the only work of man's hand that interrupted the expanse, was the schooner *Farallone*, her berth quite changed, and rocking at anchor some two miles to windward in the midst of the lagoon. The noise of the Trade ran very boisterous in all parts of the island; the nearer palm trees crashed and whistled in the gusts, those farther off contributed a humming bass like the roar of cities; and yet, to any man less absorbed, there must have risen at times over this turmoil of the winds, the sharper note of the human voice from the settlement. There all was activity. Attwater, stripped to his trousers and lending a strong hand of help, was directing and encouraging five Kanakas; from his lively voice, and their more lively efforts, it was to be gathered that some sudden and joyful emergency had set them in this bustle; and the Union Jack floated once more on its staff. But the suppliant on the beach, unconscious of their voices, prayed on with instancy and fervour, and the sound of his voice rose and fell again, and his countenance brightened and was deformed with changing moods of piety and terror.

Before his closed eyes, the skiff had been for some time tacking towards the distant and deserted *Farallone*; and presently the figure of Herrick might have been observed to board her, to pass for a while into the house, thence forward to the forecastle, and at last to plunge into the main hatch. In all these quarters, his visit was followed by a coil of smoke; and he had scarce entered his boat again and shoved off, before flames broke forth upon the schooner. They burned gaily; kerosene had not been spared, and the bellows of the Trade incited the conflagration. About half way on the return voyage, when Herrick looked back, he beheld the *Farallone* wrapped to the topmasts in leaping arms of fire, and the voluminous smoke pursuing him along the face of the lagoon. In one hour's time, he computed, the waters would have closed over the stolen ship.

It so chanced that, as his boat flew before the wind with much vivacity, and his eyes were continually busy in the wake, measuring the progress of the flames, he found himself embayed to the northward of the point of palms, and here became aware at the same time of the figure of Davis immersed in his devotion. An exclamation, part of annoyance, part of amusement, broke from him: and he touched the helm and ran the prow upon the beach not twenty feet from the unconscious devotee. Taking the painter in his hand, he landed, and drew near, and stood over him. And still the voluble and incoherent stream of prayer continued unabated. It was not possible for him to overhear the suppliant's petitions, which he listened to some while in a very mingled mood of humour and pity: and it was only when his own name began to occur and to be conjoined with epithets, that he at last laid his hand on the captain's shoulder.

'Sorry to interrupt the exercise,' said he; 'but I want you to look at the *Farallone*.'

The captain scrambled to his feet, and stood gasping and staring. 'Mr Herrick, don't startle a man like that!' he said. 'I don't seem someways rightly myself since . . .' he broke off. 'What did you say anyway? O, the *Farallone*,' and he looked languidly out.

'Yes,' said Herrick. 'There she burns! and you may guess from that what the news is.'

'The *Trinity Hall*, I guess,' said the captain.

'The same,' said Herrick; 'sighted half an hour ago, and coming up hand over fist.'

'Well, it don't amount to a hill of beans,' said the captain with a sigh.

'O, come, that's rank ingratitude!' cried Herrick.

'Well,' replied the captain, meditatively, 'you mayn't just see the way that I view it in, but I'd 'most rather stay here upon this island. I found peace here, peace in believing. Yes, I guess this island is about good enough for John Davis.'

'I never heard such nonsense!' cried Herrick. 'What! with all turning out in your favour the way it does, the *Farallone* wiped out, the crew disposed of, a sure thing for your wife and family, and you, yourself, Attwater's spoiled darling and pet penitent!'

'Now, Mr Herrick, don't say that,' said the captain gently; 'when you know he don't make no difference between us. But, O! why not be one of us? why not come to Jesus right away, and let's meet in yon beautiful land? That's just the one thing wanted; just say, Lord, I believe, help thou mine unbelief! And He'll fold you in His arms. You see, I know! I've been a sinner myself!'

NOTES

p. 8 Eimeo: one of the Society Islands.

p. 8 *sortes*: the *sortes virgilianae* ('Virgilian lots'), a method of divination by opening Virgil's *Aeneid* at random and finding what is said on the open page.

p. 13 *Freischütz*: *Der Freischütz* ('The Freeshooter'), opera by Carl Maria von Weber with a libretto by Friedrich Kind first performed in 1821.

p. 13 Kaspar: a legendary character who, having sold his soul to the Devil, cannot be redeemed unless he brings somebody else into the Devil's clutches.

p. 14 Point Venus: near Papeete. Captain Cook so named it because he used it in his voyage of 1765 when observing the passage of the planet Venus across the sun.

p. 15 B. and S.: brandy and soda.

p. 15 jarvey: hackney coachman.

p. 15 growler: four-wheeled cab.

p. 16 ulster: heavy double-breasted overcoat.

p. 20 Sachems: Indian chiefs (from Narragansett *sachim*, chief).

p. 21 'We twa hae paidled in the burn' etc.: Fourth stanza of Burns's 'Auld Lang Syne'.

p. 23 Portland: port in SW Maine, in Casco Bay (not, as is made clear later, the Portland in Oregon).

p. 25 *Einst, O wunder*: ('Once, O wonder'), from the poem 'Adelaide' by the German poet Friedrich von Matthisson (1761–1831). This poem was made famous by Beethoven's setting of it, and as a song it was a favourite of Stevenson's: he refers to it several times in his letters and in his essay 'On Falling in Love' (in *Virginibus Puerisque*).

p. 28 the Fifth Symphony: Beethoven's. The opening bars have been described as 'Fate knocking at the door'.

p. 28 *memor querela*: cf. Horace, *Odes*, III, xi,

> *et nostri memorem sepulcro*
> *scalpe querellam*

and carve upon my tomb an elegy in memory of me.

p. 28 *terque quaterque* etc.: *Aeneid I*, lines 93–6,

> *o terque quaterque beati*
> *quis ante ora patrum Troiae sub moenibus altis*
> *contigit oppetere.*

Thrice and four times blessed are those whose lot it is to die in the presence of their fathers under the high walls of Troy.

p. 28 *Ich trage unerträgliches*: 'I bear the unbearable'. The reference is to lyric XXIV in Heine's *Die Heimkehr* ('The Return Home'). Herrick is remembering the whole poem:

> *Ich unglücksel'ger Atlas! eine Welt,*
> *Die ganze Welt der Schmerzen, muss ich tragen*
> *Ich trage Unerträgliches, und brechen*
> *Will mir das Herz in Leibe.*
>
> *Du stolzes Herz! du hast es ja gewollt!*
> *Du wolltest glücklich sein, unendlich glücklich*
> *Oder unendlich elend, stolzes Herz,*
> *Und jetzo bist du elend.*

Literally:

> 'I, unhappy Atlas, a world,
> The whole world of sorrows, must I bear,
> I bear the unbearable, and want to break
> The heart in my body.
>
> You, proud heart! You indeed wished it!
> You wanted to be happy, endlessly happy,
> Or endlessly wretched, proud heart,
> And now you are wretched.

p. 31 Paumotus: see Introduction.

p. 37 *Ohé la goëlette*: Schooner ahoy.

p. 55 Ranaka and Ratiu . . . Takume and Honden: Tuamotu atolls.

p. 66 Callao: port in Peru.

p. 66 lazarette: store-room between the decks of a ship.

p. 70 Findlay: Alexander Findlay, *A Directory for the Navigation of the South Pacific*, 5th edition, London 1884. Stevenson to Charles Baxter from Sydney, 10 April, 1890: 'Persons with friends in the islands should purchase Findlay's *Pacific Directories*: they're the best of reading anyway, and may almost count as fiction.'

p. 82 'For my voice ...': nobody has succeeded in identifying this quotation, and it has been suggested that Stevenson may have invented it.

p. 90 *nemorosa Zacynthos* etc.: see Introduction.

p. 93 'And darkness was the burier of the dead': Shakespeare, *Henry IV Part II*, I, 160, 'And darkness be the burier of the dead'.

p. 104 Kingsmills: a group of islands, part of the Gilbert Islands.

p. 117 Laputa: in Part III of Swift's *Gulliver's Travels* the people of Laputa are so preoccupied with theoretical speculations that they cannot cope with the practicalities of everyday life.

p. 121 Noumea: capital and chief port of the French Overseas Territory of New Caledonia, which had a penal colony.

p. 133 Shykespeare or the musical glasses: Goldsmith, *Vicar of Wakefield*, '... with other fashionable topics, such as pictures, taste, Shakespeare, and the musical glasses.' But surely it is out of character for Huish to refer to this?

p. 133 Tophet: in the Old Testament a place in the valley south-west of Jerusalem where human sacrifices had been offered to Moloch, hence a symbol of Hell and its torments.

SUGGESTIONS FOR FURTHER READING

J. C. Furnas, *Voyage to Windward*, 1951. This is the classic modern biography of Stevenson, which restored the true Stevenson after earlier idolatries and debunkings. It is especially good on Stevenson and the South Seas.

Jenni Calder, *R. L. S.: A Life Study*, 1980. A sensitive study of Stevenson's life, work and character.

David Daiches, *Robert Louis Stevenson and His World*, 1973. Sets Stevenson in his time and place.

The Letters of Robert Louis Stevenson were edited by Sidney Colvin in two volumes in 1899, but this edition is far from complete.

Stevenson's Letters to Charles Baxter were edited by DeLancey Ferguson and Marshall Waingrow in 1956. These letters contain some of R. L. S.'s most vivid and uninhibited personal writings.

Stevenson was a marvellous letter writer. His complete letters are at last to be published by Yale University Press in eight volumes after many years of patient research by Bradford A. Booth and Ernest Mehew. The first two of these volumes appeared in 1994. When complete, this edition will contain nearly 2,800 letters of which only 1,100 have been previously published.

The reader might want to compare Stevenson's treatment of the white man in the tropics with that of Joseph Conrad (as suggested in the Introduction). Conrad's *Youth, Heart of Darkness* and *The End of the Tether* are available in a single volume in Everyman Paperbacks, as is another relevant Conrad novel, *Victory*.

CLASSIC FICTION
IN EVERYMAN

A SELECTION

Frankenstein
MARY SHELLEY
A masterpiece of Gothic terror in its
original 1818 version **£3.99**

Dracula
BRAM STOKER
One of the best known horror stories
in the world **£3.99**

The Diary of A Nobody
GEORGE AND WEEDON
GROSSMITH
A hilarious account of suburban life
in Edwardian London **£4.99**

Some Experiences
and Further Experiences
of an Irish R. M.
SOMERVILLE AND ROSS
Gems of comic exuberance and
improvisation **£4.50**

Three Men in a Boat
JEROME K. JEROME
English humour at its best **£2.99**

Twenty Thousand Leagues
under the Sea
JULES VERNE
Scientific fact combines with
fantasy in this prophetic tale of
underwater adventure **£4.99**

The Best of Father Brown
G. K. CHESTERTON
An irresistible selection of crime
stories – unique to Everyman **£4.99**

The Collected Raffles
E. W. HORNUNG
Dashing exploits from the most glam-
orous figure in crime fiction **£4.99**

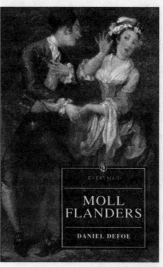

£5.99